SPECTACULAR CARS OF HONG KONG

An *Instacar*HK *Journey*

經典的魅力

*Instacar*HK 試駕之旅

Justin Lui · 呂璟豪

To my dear wife

For her unconditional support since

the very beginning of this journey

(including being the sole camerawoman

for a few of the reviews!)

致愛妻

感謝妳從這段旅程最初

就給予我無條件的支持，

包括在一些評測中擔任唯一的攝影師！

Table of contents

目錄

Preface 前言

Thanks to growing up in a family full of car guys, I have been a petrol head since before I can remember. My passion slowly shifted to classic cars as I grew older and, before I know it, I became an active member of the Classic Car Club of Hong Kong (the oldest car club in Hong Kong founded in 1979). One day, during casual drinks with some of my closest buddies from the Club, I realised the majority of them were in the media business. I therefore got the idea that we should start a YouTube channel to review classic cars. And that was the birth of InstacarHK – an automotive multimedia platform for like-minded individuals with a passion for cars.

The intention of this book is to create a physical time capsule of the memories from all the great cars we reviewed and all the fun we had in the process. The interesting thing is I actually had the idea of publishing a book on classic cars before I had the idea of starting a YouTube channel. Fate decided that the channel should come first, which was very fortunate as it made the journey so much more enjoyable. And now we have come full circle.

I am extremely grateful for the team's time, dedication, and passion for the channel over the years. I am also very thankful for all the owners of the cars that we reviewed; their generosity is incredible. I hope other car lovers will enjoy this book as much as we enjoyed reviewing these truly spectacular cars.

Justin Lui

我成長於一個充滿車迷的家庭，所以自懂事以來，我就是個汽車迷。隨着年齡漸長，我的熱情逐漸轉向了老爺車，在不知不覺中，竟成為了香港老爺車會的活躍成員（該會於 1979 年成立，是香港歷史最悠久的汽車會）。有一天，我與老爺車會的好友聚會，發現他們大多數從事媒體工作。我因此萌生了一個念頭：我們應該開設一個評測老爺車的 YouTube 頻道，而這就是 InstacarHK 的誕生——一個專為志同道合、熱愛汽車的人設立的汽車多媒體平台。

出版這本書的目的是希望創造一個時間囊，以記錄所有我們評測過的優秀汽車以及過程中充滿歡樂的回憶。值得一提，其實在構思開設 YouTube 頻道之前，我就有出版老爺車書的想法。幸運地，命運趨生了這個頻道，令整個計劃變得更完整，過程也更愉快。現在我們又實踐了原本的構思。

我非常感謝團隊多年來為頻道付出的時間、努力和熱情。我同時感謝所有借出汽車供我們評測的車主，他們非常慷慨，令人難以置信。我希望其他汽車迷會像我們一樣，享受閱讀這本書，並能夠感受這些令人讚嘆的汽車所帶來的歡樂。

呂璟豪

Production Years: 1986-1996
Engine: Fuel injected 5.0 V8; 400HP
Total Production: 480 units

生產年份：1986-1996
引擎：燃油噴注 5.0 V8；400 匹馬力
總產量：480 輛

Owner's remarks:

This is not a 1960s classics but a 90s "continuation" model, but it is also the last Cobra Mark IV hand-built in aluminium on the original wooden bucks. I remember how, back in 1996, I drove up to the historic Brooklands race track where the AC factory was located every Saturday morning to see the progress of the build. It was like witnessing the birth of a child.

Driving the Cobra must be one of the most visceral experiences short of skydiving: vastly over-engined (that cross-plane American muscle V8 gives a typical angry uneven beat and produces monumental power and torque) with little protection both against the elements and, god forbid, accidents. One can only admire the heroics of those who raced these cars in the 60s.

車主的話：

這輛不是 1960 年代的老爺車，而是 90 年代的「續作」型號，但也是最後一輛在原始木製架上用鋁製手工打造的 Cobra Mk IV。我還記得在 1996 年時，每個週六早上我都會開車前往 AC 工廠所在的那條歷史悠久的布魯克蘭賽道裏，觀察車輛製造的進度。就像見證小寶寶的誕生。

駕駛 Cobra 必定是除跳傘外最直觀的體驗：強大的引擎（那台橫置的「美式肌肉」V8 引擎有着典型的憤怒和不均勻的節奏，並產生巨大的動力和扭力），幾乎沒有任何應對外來環境或防止意外的保護措施。只能敬佩在 60 年代駕駛這些汽車的勇士。

AC Cobra Mk IV (1996)

AC Cars was a British sports car company that was founded since 1901 and was no stranger to making sports cars that ruled the racetracks. In 1961, legendary American race car driver Carroll Shelby approached AC Cars and asked if they could build him a car that he can fit an American V8 engine into. In the meantime, Ford offered Shelby their new lightweight "Windsor" V8 engine. A legend was born and the Cobra went on to enjoy a very successful racing career, cementing its position forever in the hall of fame of eminent sports cars.

The Mk IV has a pretty interesting history of its own too. By the 1970s, AC Cars had already stopped servicing and producing the Cobra. One of their employees who was responsible for the Cobra line, Brian Angliss, left the company and set up his own shop to service and restore Cobras. Due to Brian's knowledge with the model, he quickly made a reputation for himself as the man to go to for these cars. In particular, Brian was able to purchase original Cobra tooling, parts, and moulds from AC Cars factory thanks to his relationship with them, making his work on the cars ever so authentic. By the 1980s, Brian's Cobra business was so successful that he decided to incorporate a new company called AutoKraft, a joint venture with Ford, and started producing the Mk IV Cobra. By 1986, he was also able to acquire the trade name AC Cars when the company went into liquidation and hence the genuine, legitimate "AC Cobra" was reborn, in the form of the Mk IV. AutoKraft continued to build the Mk IV until 1996, when it too, was unable

AC 汽車是一家於 1901 年成立的英國跑車公司，其生產的跑車在賽道上稱霸已是人所共知。1961 年，傳奇美國賽車手 Carroll Shelby 要求 AC 汽車為他製造一輛安裝美式 V8 引擎的汽車。與此同時，福特向 Shelby 提供了一台新型輕量化「溫莎」V8 引擎。傳奇就此誕生了，Cobra 在賽車界取得了非凡的成就，長久地鞏固了它在傑出跑車名人堂中的地位。

Mk IV 本身也有一段相當有趣的歷史。到了 1970 年代，AC 汽車已經停止維修及生產 Cobra。其中一名負責 Cobra 生產線的員工 Brian Angliss 離開了公司，並自立門戶來維修和修復 Cobra。由於 Brian 對這款車的了解，他很快成了專家，變得聲名大噪，每當人們尋求 Cobra 時都會想起他。由於 Brian 與 AC 汽車工廠的關係，他能夠從 AC 汽車工廠購買原廠 Cobra 工具、零件和模具，使他修復這些車的工作變得更加正宗。到了 1980 年代，Brian 的 Cobra 業務非常成功，他決定與福特共同成立一家新公司，名為 AutoKraft，開始生產 Mk IV Cobra。到了 1986 年，AC 汽車公司破產時，他甚至取得「AC 汽車」商標的使用權，使正統的

to avoid the demise of its predecessors and went into liquidation. AutoKraft made a total of 480 Mk IV Cobras, the one we are showing here being one of the last ones made in 1996.

This particular car went through quite a bit of a roller coaster throughout its life. Kept by the same owner since new, the car was first enjoyed around English B roads before being brought back to Hong Kong a few years later. In 2014, during one of Hong Kong's mega typhoons, the owner's home garage was completely flooded, drowning the Cobra and taking along with it an Aston Martin DB9 Volante and a Ferrari 458 Spider. While the latter two can be written off, the owner rightfully did not have the heart to do the same with the Cobra, and decided to send it back to the UK to a specialist called Dragonwheels for a thorough restoration – which took 7 years!

The car today is in all original spec except for one thing – the engine. As expected, the drowned engine could not be salvaged, therefore a similar 5.0L Ford V8 engine was sourced from another specialist, Knights Engineering. This engine is, however, race-tuned and produces a mind-blowing 400HP versus the original 250HP.

That engine, truly takes the cake. I have driven a number of American V8's before but none sounded so aggressively intoxicating. It is loud, and in an open cockpit the sound consumes pretty much the entire driving atmosphere. Perhaps it is because this engine is no ordinary Ford engine but a race-tuned one, but it just urges you to step on it at every opportunity, and step on it I did. It revs freely to redline and really shifts the car. The torque is also incredible and what gear you are in at any given time is totally irrelevant, for the car just goes when you step on it. Thanks to the powerful engine and the extremely lightweight, the car simply flies. A truly fantastic car and I dare say the best "American muscle" I have ever driven.

「AC Cobra」能合法地以 Mk IV 的形式重新誕生。AutoKraft 一直繼續生產 Mk IV，但直到 1996 年，它也無法避免破產的命運。AutoKraft 總共生產了 480 輛 Mk IV Cobra，而我們在這裏展示的是在 1996 年生產其中的最後一輛。

這輛汽車背後有一段相當曲折的故事。自從新車時起，一直由同一位車主保管，最初在英國的郊野道路上行駛，幾年後被帶回香港。2014 年，在香港一場超級颱風期間，車主的私人車房完全被水淹浸，Cobra、阿斯頓‧馬丁 DB9 Volante 和法拉利 458 Spider 全數損壞。後兩者最終報廢，但車主無法這樣對待 Cobra，於是決定將它送回英國，由名為 Dragonwheels 的專家進行全面修復，這花了整整七年的時間！

現在這輛車完全回復原始規格，除了引擎是例外。不出所料，被淹浸的引擎無法修復，因此車主從另一個專家 Knights Engineering 找到了一個類似的 5.0 公升福特 V8 引擎。然而，這款引擎經過調校，產生了驚人的 400 匹馬力，相比原的 250 匹馬力有了巨大的提升。

這個引擎確實讓人驚艷。我以前駕駛過幾款美式 V8 引擎汽車，但沒有一個聽起來如此令人陶醉。它聲音很大，在開篷車廂中，引擎的聲音幾乎佔據了整個車廂。也許因為它不是普通的福特引擎，而是經過調校的，它總是鼓動你不惜一切踩上油門，而我確實踩了上去。它自由轉速到紅線區域，真的能讓車子飛馳。扭力也非常驚人，在任何時候轉波都完全無關緊要，一踩油門車子就飛馳而去。憑藉強大的引擎和輕盈的車身，這輛車簡直就像能飛一般。真是一輛了不起的汽車，我敢説它是我駕駛過最優秀的「美式肌肉車」。

Production Years: 1990-2005
Engine: Fuel injected 3.0 V6; 280HP
Total Production: 18,000+ units

生產年份：1990-2005
引擎：燃油噴注 3.0 V6；280 匹馬力
總產量：超過 18,000 輛

Owner's remarks:

The NSX was a love at first sight for me. Its looks, technology, and racing pedigree are what I am most attracted to. To me, this car is more than a car – it is art – and I therefore treat it as such.

車主的話：

NSX 對我來說是一見鍾情。它的外觀、科技和賽車血統是最吸引我的地方。對我來說，這輛車不僅僅是一輛汽車——它是一件藝術品——因此我也是如此對待它。

Acura 極品
NSX (1994)

The NSX really needs no introduction. It made headlines as the Ferrari challenger when it was released in the early 1990s, and a legitimate challenger it was. Coded as "HP-X" for "Honda Pininfarina eXperimental", the NSX project was first introduced during the 1980s, when Honda was providing racing engines to the McLaren F1 racing team that was running away with the championship year after year with their two legendary drivers Aryton Senna and Alain Prost. Honda decided that they should make use of the racing technology they had at the time and produce a supercar for road use.

Equipped with a 3.0 V6 naturally aspirated V-Tec engine with 280HP, the NSX might not look like a competitive supercar on paper even for the early 1990s, but it is what is underneath that matters. The chassis and body panels were made in aluminium, something even Ferrari did not do until 1999 with the 360 Modena. The V-Tec engine uses high-tech materials like titanium connecting rods. The chassis was also pedantically tuned – including involvement and input by the great Aryton Senna. The result was a 1,370KG supercar with a high revving and punchy engine. The chassis is so good that Gordon Murray openly admitted he used the NSX's chassis as reference for his design of the McLaren F1 road car.

The NSX we are showing here is an Acura, which simply means it was an export version and not a Japanese domestic version (Honda uses the brand Acura for export markets as the latter is considered to be more prestigious, just like the Toyota and Lexus relationship). This NSX is known to be the cleanest and neatest NSX in Hong Kong because it has won

NSX 真的不需要太多介紹。在 1990 年代初發佈時，它以法拉利的挑戰者成為了頭條新聞，而且它是一個真正的競爭對手。以「HP-X」（「Honda Pininfarina eXperimental」的簡稱）當代號為 NSX 的項目首次在 1980 年代推出時，本田正向依靠傳奇賽車手 Aryton Senna 和 Alain Prost 而屢獲世界冠軍的麥拿倫一級方程式賽車隊提供賽車引擎。本田決定利用當時的賽車技術生產一款在公路行駛的超級跑車。

即使 NSX 配備一台 3.0 公升自然進氣 V-Tec V6 引擎，擁有 280 匹馬力，在 1990 年代初，它看起來可能並不是一輛具競爭力的超級跑車，但它的內在潛力更重要。底盤和車身都是鋁製的，這是法拉利在 1999 年的 360 Modena 之前都還沒有採用的材料。V-Tec 引擎使用高科技材料，如鈦合金連桿。底盤也進行了精心調校——加入了傳奇賽車手 Aryton Senna 的建議。結果造成了一輛 1,370 公斤重並配備高轉速和強力的引擎的超級跑車。因為底盤十分優秀，以至 Gordon Murray 公開承認他曾以 NSX 的底盤作為他設計麥拿倫一級方程式的參考。

multiple awards from the Classic Car Club of Hong Kong's annual Chater Road Show Concours. In 2019, it won the "Best of Show" award which is normally reserved for classics like the Ferrari 288 GTO or Lamborghini Miura – a Japanese modern classic winner is certainly an incredible feat.

To keep a car so clean and original requires a lot of effort and sacrifice. The car has had a full dealer service record for most of its life; it has always been driven scarcely, and obviously never in the rain. OCD-behaviours by the owner include: never wearing jeans to drive it to avoid scratching the interior leather, avoiding highways to avoid stone chips and, this is my favourite, avoiding driving at night so that he does not have to turn on the headlights so as to prevent the clear lenses from turning yellow.

The car has an automatic gearbox so performance inevitably lacks a bit compared to a manual. The fact that the car is driven so little also means the engine is not in its top form (a common price to pay for low-mileage time capsule cars) – it has only clocked around 40,000KM (approx. 25,000 miles) in 26 years. However, you instantly recognise that the NSX means business the minute you sit in it. The sound from its V6 engine is a lot more potent than its JDM contemporaries; the chassis and suspension set up feels serious and firm, but not uncomfortable. Its size is sensible (unlike cars of today), making it a sophisticated and efficient car to throw around mountain roads.

I am very grateful to finally be able to try out the legendary NSX after hearing about how special it is for so many years. It did not disappoint.

在這裏展示的 NSX 是一輛極品版本，意味着它是出口的，而不是日本國內的版本（本田在外銷市場使用極品品牌，被認為更有威望，就像豐田和凌志的關係）。這輛 NSX 被譽為香港最企理和最整潔的 NSX，因為它曾多次獲得香港老爺車會的年度中環遮打道老爺車展選美比賽的獎項。在 2019 年，它獲得了一般是法拉利 288 GTO 或林寶堅尼 Miura 等老爺車的囊中物的全場大獎，一輛日本現代老爺車能獲得此獎絕對是一項驚人的成就。

要能把車子保持得如此企理和原始，需要很多努力和犧牲。車子一生中大部份時間都保留了完整的經銷商維修紀錄；車主很少駕駛它，當然也從不在雨中行駛。車主有着強迫症般的行為，例如：開車時從不穿牛仔褲，以免刮傷內部皮革；避免上高速公路以免被石子擊中；而這是我最喜歡的一點：他避免在夜間駕駛，以免開啟車頭燈使透明鏡片變黃。

由於車子配備自動波箱，其性能無可避免會較手動波箱差一些。車子鮮少駕駛也意味着引擎難以處於最佳狀態（這是低里數老爺車的普遍代價）——它在 26 年裏只行駛了約 40,000 公里（約 25,000 英里）。然而，一旦你坐進 NSX 裏，你立刻就會意識到它的意義非凡。V6 引擎的聲音比同期的日本車更加強烈；底盤和避震設定感覺沉重而穩健，但並不會令人不適。它的車身尺寸很合理（不像現今的車輛），使它成為一輛能在山路上飛馳的高效清湛的汽車。

我很多年前已聽說過 NSX 有多麼特別，很感恩終於能夠體驗傳奇的 NSX。它沒有讓我失望。

Production Years: 1971-1975
Engine: Fuel injected 3.0 inline-6; 200HP
Total Production: 8,359 units

生產年份：1971-1975
引擎：燃油噴注 3.0 直列 6 缸；200 匹馬力
總產量：8,359 輛

Owner's remarks:

I had not seen one of these beautiful old Bimmers until I was 20, by which time most of them had already infamously rusted away. I was gobsmacked by its sexy profile as it roared passed me. It was love at first sight!

Years later I finally got to have one of my own and it has been a thrilling 12 years of ownership. I still cannot keep my eyes off her.

車主的話：

在我 20 歲前，還沒見過這種華麗的老爺寶馬，而當時大多數車輛已經出現鏽蝕，人盡皆爺。當它在我身旁轟鳴而過時，我被它性感的輪廓震懾了。這可算是一見鍾情！

多年後，我終於擁有了自己的寶馬，12 年後我仍然無法將目光從它身上移開。

BMW 寶馬
3.0 CSi (1973)

The BMW we are reviewing here is a 1973 3.0 CSi. Known internally as the "E9", BMW first introduced the model in 1968 in the form of the 2800 CS. In 1971, BMW introduced the 3.0 CS and 3.0 CSi models, both having a 3 litre, inline 6, single overhead cam engine. The difference being that the 3.0 CS had carburettors and produced 180 HP while the 3.0 CSi was fuel injected and produced 200 HP (hence the "i" [injection] in the name CSi).

Most people who are unfamiliar with classic BMW's do not know much about the CSi, as all their focus would be on the CSL model – the limited and lightweight homologation version of the E9 that BMW released in its bid to join the Group 2 European Touring Car Championship back in the 1970s. The CSL was actually based on the CSi, but it shaved off 210KG by using thinner body panels and aluminium for certain body parts like the engine bonnet. The engine was based on the 3.0 CSi with only a slight increase in engine capacity from 2,986cc to 3,153cc. Power output was therefore only a handful more than the CSi. This shows the racing pedigree and importance of the 3.0 CSi, for without it, there could arguably be no CSL, the race car that won multiple European Touring Car Championship titles in the 1970s.

Sitting in the car, one immediately feels the typical 1970s vibe with very good visibility, thanks to the ultra-thin A and C pillars, the seats are typical 1970s fabric, and there are lots of wood in the cabin. The car is easy to start as it is fuel injected; and despite being fuel injected, the engine note still sounds potent and thick. The clutch is not particularly heavy; the gear shift is tight and precise, although because it is a four-speed manual, the gears are noticeably long. One thing that needs getting used to is

　　我們在這裏評測的寶馬是 1973 年款的 3.0 CSi。寶馬於 1968 年首次推出 2800 CS 型號，內部稱為「E9」。1971 年，寶馬推出了 3.0 CS 和 3.0 CSi 型號，兩者均配備 3 公升直列 6 缸單頂置凸輪軸引擎。不同之處在於 3.0 CS 安裝了化油器，輸出功率為 180 匹馬力，而 3.0 CSi 則採用了燃油噴注系統，輸出功率達到了 200 匹馬力（因此名稱中有「i」，代表 injection）。

　　不太熟悉老爺寶馬的人，多數也不太了解 CSi，因為他們都把焦點放在 CSL 型號上——E9 的限量版和輕量化型號，這是寶馬在 1970 年代為加入歐洲房車錦標賽第二組而發佈的。CSL 實際上是建基於 CSi 的，但它通過使用較薄的車身板和鋁製引擎蓋等部件而削減了 210 公斤的重量。引擎依據 3.0 CSi，僅稍微使排氣量從 2,986 cc 增加到 3,153 cc。因此，動力輸出僅稍高於 CSi。這反映 3.0 CSi 的賽車血統和重要性，如果沒有它，也許在 1970 年代曾贏得多次歐洲房車錦標賽冠軍的 CSL 就不會出現了。

　　坐在車內，你立刻感受到典型的 1970 年代氣氛，視野非常良好，這歸功於超薄的 A 柱和 C 柱，座椅是典型的 1970 年代物料，車內有大量木製裝飾。由於採用了燃油噴注系統，車子很容易啟動，

the throttle. It is quite hard and sticky, and you need to confidently step on it all the way down when you try to set off from a standstill. Once on the road, the car feels good and comfortable with very reasonable suspension travel. At about 1,400KG, it is not a light car, and since it does not have a lazy V8 engine, it is not particularly torquey either. However, once you get the momentum going, the car is reasonably quick and takes corners firmly and confidently. BMW's claim of being "the ultimate driving machine" was clearly evident since very early on.

There are not many E9's left in this world as many have rusted away (there is a recurring joke that coachbuilder Karmann put the car together with the rust on since day one), and they are certainly rare in Hong Kong. We are very blessed that the owner of this E9 uses it regularly and brings it out to all Classic Car Club events.

儘管如此，引擎的聲音聽起來仍然強而有力。離合器並不特別沉重；轉波緊湊而精確，不過由於是四速手動波箱，波段的間距相對較長。需要適應的是油門——它相當硬而有些卡滯，當你從靜止狀態啟動車子時，你需要使勁地將油門踩到底。在路上，車子感覺良好而舒適，避震行程非常合理。它重約1,400 公斤，絕不輕盈，而由於它沒有惰性的 V8 引擎，扭力並不特別強勁。然而，一旦你保持動力，車子的加速相當快，並且能夠自信而穩固地應對彎道，充份體現寶馬「極致駕駛機器」的宣傳口號。

世界上的 E9 已不多，許多都已經鏽蝕（有一個流傳已久的笑話是，車身製造商 Karmann 從一開始就採用生鏽的零件組裝這輛車），在香港確實也非常罕見。我們非常幸運，這輛 E9 的車主經常駕駛它，並將它帶到香港老爺車會的所有活動中亮相。

Production Years: 1973-1982
Engine: Carburetted 5.7 V8; 200HP
Total Production (for the convertible models made in 1973 only): 4,943 units

生產年份：1973-1982
引擎：化油器 5.7 V8；200 匹馬力
總產量（僅限於 1973 年生產的敞篷車型）：4,943 輛

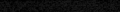

Owner's remarks:

Growing up I loved two cars, the original Lamborghini Countach and the Corvette Stingray. Their shapes, whilst vastly different, seemed so exotic vs. the boxy shapes of the everyday cars in the 1980s. My career took me to the USA and shortly after arriving I realised my dream of owning a Corvette. I love the curves and shapes the designers could achieve using fibreglass, the long bonnet and the rumble from the V8 engine.

車主的話：

在成長過程中，我喜歡兩輛車，一輛是原始的林寶堅尼 Countach，另一輛是雪佛蘭 Stingray。它們的外形雖然大相徑庭，但與 1980 年代方盒子形狀的普通車輛相比，顯得十分奇特。我因為工作關係來到美國，不久就實現了擁有一輛 Corvette 的夢想。我喜歡設計師使用玻璃纖維所展現的曲線和形狀，以及它修長的引擎蓋和 V8 引擎的轟隆聲響。

Chevrolet 雪佛蘭 Corvette C3 (1973)

I have had reasonable exposure to different classic cars before, especially since we launched the InstacarHK YouTube channel where generous owners frequently let me test drive their beautiful cars. However, this review is extra-special as it is my first time ever experiencing an American classic, or rather an American muscle. I do not think I have ever even sat in one before, so to go straight to driving one is truly a day to remember.

What we are showing here is a 1973 Chevrolet Corvette convertible in a beautiful golden orange colour. It is a 350 cubic inch "small block" V8. For non-American car enthusiasts who would, like me, have no idea what 350 cubic inch means, it actually means 5.7 litres (1 cubic inch = 0.0164 litres). The car has 200HP, which is not sufficient, but more on that later. The first Corvette model, the "C1", was introduced in 1953. The model we have here is the "C3", which is the third-generation model and was produced between 1968 and 1982.

This particular C3, being a 1973 model, is quite special. 1973 was the first year that Chevrolet had to give up the chrome front bumpers on their Corvettes and replace them with plastic ones due to new pedestrian safety laws. 1973 was also the only year in which the Corvette had front plastic bumpers but the rear chrome bumpers remained, making it a "half & half" car, visually. From 1974 onwards, the rear bumpers of all Corvettes were replaced with plastic ones.

Chevrolet made a little less than 5,000 units of the 1973 Chevrolet Corvette convertible. The one we have here being a convertible, manual, and with factory

我之前曾接觸不少老爺車，特別是自我們開設了 InstacarHK YouTube 頻道後，慷慨的車主們經常讓我試駕他們華麗的汽車。然而，這次評測對我來說非常特別，因為是我第一次體驗美國的老爺車，或者更準確地說，是「美式肌肉車」。我從來沒有坐過這種車，所以這次試駕非常值得紀念。

這是一輛塗上漂亮金橙色的 1973 年雪佛蘭 Corvette 敞篷車。它有一個 350 立方英寸「小方塊」V8 引擎。對於像我這種不太熱衷於美國車的車迷來說，可能不知道 350 立方英寸是甚麼意思，實際上它等如 5.7 公升的容量（1 立方英寸 =0.0164 公升）。這輛車擁有 200 匹馬力，不算大，這點稍後再談。第一輛 Corvette 車型「C1」於 1953 年推出。這輛是「C3」車型，屬第三代車型，於 1968 年至 1982 年間生產。

這輛特殊的 C3 屬 1973 年型號，相當特別。新的行人安全法規於 1973 年實施，雪佛蘭首次放棄其 Corvette 的鉻合金前保險槓，並更換為塑料保險槓。該年也是 Corvette 採用塑料前保險槓但保留鉻合金後保險槓的唯一一年，使其在視覺上成為「一半一半」的車型。從 1974 年開始，所有 Corvette 車型的後保險槓都改用塑料材質。

雪佛蘭生產了不到 5,000 輛 1973 年型號的 Corvette 敞篷車。這次評測的敞篷車，有手動波箱並配有原廠空調，使它屬於較罕見的車型。特別之處，是這輛車乃選配了「豪華硬頂」選項的 323 輛車之一，意思是它帶有一個原廠可拆卸硬頂。

當我第一次坐進車內時，我立刻感覺到它是多麼小巧玲瓏。另一件值得留意的是儀表盤——它們從方向盤下方向下延伸，當你想看一眼車速表和轉速表時，感覺就像在俯視懸崖。啟動車輛時，離合器和油門踏板的行程正常，易於適應，只是需要更使勁踩油門才能啟動。四速手動波箱的轉波敏捷而

air-conditioning puts it on the rarer side of the scale. This is especially the case given this particular car is only one of 323 units that have been optioned with the "Deluxe Hard Top" option, which basically means it comes with a factory detachable hardtop.

When I first sat in the car, I immediately noticed how small it is. Another thing is the dials – they descend downwards from the steering wheel so it feels like you are looking down a cliff when trying to get a glimpse of the speedometer and tachometer. When setting off, the clutch and gas pedals' respective travels are normal and easy to adapt to, although more gas is needed to set off. The gear change of the four-speed manual gearbox is short and precise.

The car sounds like what you would expect from an American V8, although it is quieter than I have anticipated. The car's lack of power is quite evident, although the torque helps a little. Being a left-hand drive car, it naturally takes some time to get used to when driving it in Hong Kong. However, this is where the car's compact size really helps.

All in all, my first experience with an American classic did not disappoint. A more powerful example, perhaps a "big block" of some sort, may have provided a more American muscle experience, but this car's size and delightful gear changes compensate for any lack of power. Its size, colour, and open top layout make it a fun little car to drive around Hong Kong's country roads, which was a pleasant and much welcomed surprise.

精確。

這輛車的聲音與你所期望的美國 V8 引擎一樣，但比我預期的要安靜。儘管扭力帶來些幫助，但車子的動力明顯不足，作為左軚車，在香港駕駛它確實需要一些時間適應。不過，這輛車的小巧尺寸適合在香港駕駛。

總括而言，我第一次駕駛美國老爺車的體驗並沒有讓我失望。如果可以試駕一輛更大馬大的車，也許是某種「大方塊」引擎的型號，或許能夠給我更具「美式肌肉車」的駕駛體驗，但這輛車的尺寸和敏捷的轉波彌補了其動力不足的弱點。它的尺寸、顏色和敞篷設計使它成為一輛在香港郊野道路上穿梭的有趣小巧汽車，那是一個令人愉快的驚喜體驗。

Production Years (for the Series II only): 1965-1967
Engine: Carburetted 4.0 V12; 300HP
Total Production (for the Series II only): 455 units

生產年份（僅限於 Series II）：1965-1967
引擎：化油器 4.0 V12；300 匹馬力
總產量（僅限於 Series II）：455 輛

Owner's remarks:

Every Colombo V12 is special, and that includes the milder triple downdraft version in the 330GT. I like Grand Touring cars and this one hits the spot. It is solidly built and reliable, the exhaust note is subdued but still easily recognisable as the sound of a V12 from Maranello. A wonderful time machine to bring one back to the swinging Sixties.

車主的話：

每一輛安裝 Colombo V12 引擎的車都與別不同，包括 330GT 中較溫和的三重下吸式版本。我喜歡大型豪華巡航跑車，而這一款正合我意。它結實耐用，排氣聲音低沉，但仍然能清楚地辨認出為來自 Maranello 的 V12 引擎。這是一台能將人帶回六十年代的美妙時光機。

Ferrari 法拉利
330 GT 2+2 Series II (1966)

To review any Ferrari is a special occasion. Inevitably, however, some are more special than others, especially if it is a vintage model with the legendary "Colombo" V12 engine. The car in question? A 1966 Ferrari 330 GT 2+2. Part of the traditional four-seater V12 Ferrari model range, which was actually Enzo Ferrari's personal favourite, the lineage first began in mass production with the Ferrari 250 GTE in 1960. In 1965, Ferrari released the Series II 330 GT 2+2, the subject car, which is largely the same as the Series I 330 GT 2+2 that precedes it, except it has a better-looking frontend with Ferrari's classic dual headlight layout.

Named the 330 under Ferrari's traditional model designation method, it has 330cc capacity per cylinder, 12 of which makes it a 4 litre V12 with three downdraft carburettors. Its legendary Colombo engine is a race-car-derived engine designed by Gioacchino Colombo, who first worked at Alfa Romeo's F1 racing team with Enzo Ferrari before moving over to Ferrari where it all began.

Slotting the gear stick of the H-gate transmission into first gear proves to be extremely precise and solid. The clutch, while on the heavy side, is manageable and easy to modulate when setting off from standstill. There is no power steering, however, and manoeuvring the car in standstill is a real workout since the steering is ultra heavy.

Readers who have experienced in person or through YouTube videos the unique and magnificent sound of Colombo engine legends like the 250 GTO or 250 SWB would no doubt understand my anticipation to have my mind blown when I stepped down on the

評測任何一輛法拉利都是特別的體驗。老實說，有些型號的確與眾不同，尤其如果它是一輛配有傳奇「Colombo」V12引擎的老爺車。這輛是甚麼車？這就是一輛1966年的法拉利330 GT 2+2。這是傳統的四座位V12法拉利車型系列的一部份，亦是Enzo Ferrari個人最喜歡的車型，該系列是由1960年誕生的法拉利250 GTE型號開始大量生產的。1965年，法拉利推出了Series II的330 GT 2+2，而評測的這輛車就屬於這個版本，它與之前的Series I的330 GT 2+2幾乎相同，只是前端設計更美觀，採用了法拉利經典的雙頭燈佈局。

這輛車根據法拉利傳統的車型命名方法而被命名為330，每個汽缸容量為330cc，共有12個汽缸，使其成為一台帶有三個下吸式化油器的4公升V12引擎。其傳奇的Colombo引擎，源自Gioacchino Colombo設計的賽車引擎，他最初在Enzo Ferrari所工作的愛快·羅密歐一級方程式賽車隊工作，後來轉投Enzo Ferrari自己成立的法拉利賽車隊，而Colombo引擎的傳奇由此開始。

將H型波桿進入一波，感覺到它非常精確堅固。雖然離合器有些沉重，但從靜止啟動時仍易於控制並能逐漸加速。然而，它沒有風油軑，因此在靜止時操縱車輛相對費力。

有些讀者可能已親身體驗過或通過YouTube影片聽到傳奇Colombo引擎那獨特和壯觀的聲音，例如250 GTO或250 SWB，而毫無疑問，他們會理解我在第一次踏下油門時，對那種震撼感覺的期待。然而，必須承認，第一印象稍微遜色，引擎聲音並不如我所料的巨大或澎湃。這時我猛然想起，這輛車從未打算像其賽車出身的兩座位車型系列那樣，而是被設計成一輛豪華的大型巡航跑車，可以舒適地載着一家四口旅行歐洲度假。因此，與汽車其他部份一樣，其引擎聲音精緻而微妙，絕非喧鬧和激進。

throttle for the first time. Admittedly though, the first impression was a little short of expectation, for the engine note was not anywhere as shouty or aggressive as I had hoped. That was when I was reminded that this car was never intended to be like its race-bred, two-seater siblings. It was made to be a luxurious grand tourer that could comfortably take a family of four across Europe for family holidays. As such, as with the rest of the car, its engine note is refined and subtle, rather than loud and confrontational.

The impressive thing about this car is that everything works as it should, perfectly. There is no delay in throttle response, the gear change is crisp and accurate, there are no unnecessary pops and bangs, and the power delivery is superb without any hesitation whatsoever. There could be a reason for this. You see, this particular 330 GT 2+2 was formerly owned by automotive star Harry Metcalfe, founder of one of the world's most popular car magazine evo, and now host of his extremely popular YouTube channel, Harry's Garage. Harry told me that shortly after he acquired the car more than a decade ago, Ferrari offered to take the car into Maranello's Classiche Department for the team to have a look over. Ferrari then returned the car to Harry and the car has been in rude health since. Harry admitted, however, that to this day, he has no idea what Ferrari has done to the car.

I have had the fortunes of driving many different classic Ferrari's before, including the mighty F40. However, a vintage V12 Ferrari with a Colombo engine is certainly a bucket list item that I can now proudly put a tick next to. That, and the fact that this car's immediate previous owner was Harry Metcalfe, who was the sole inspiration to my own YouTube Channel, makes this experience extra sweet.

令人印象深刻的是，車子每個方面都完美運作。油門反應迅速，轉波動作乾脆準確，沒有多餘的爆裂聲和噪音，動力輸出出色，毫不遲滯。這可能有其原因。這輛 330 GT 2+2 以前是屬於車壇明星 Harry Metcalfe 的，他是世界上最受歡迎的汽車雜誌《evo》的創始人，現在也是極受歡迎的 YouTube 頻道 Harry's Garage 的主持人。Harry 告訴我，在十多年前他購入這輛車後不久，法拉利廠方主動提議他將車送到 Maranello 的 Classiche 部門供他們檢查。然後，法拉利將車送還 Harry，從此車子一直保持良好狀態。Harry 承認，他直到今天仍不知道法拉利對車子做了甚麼。

我有幸駕駛過許多不同的經典法拉利，包括強大的 F40。然而，安裝了 Colombo 引擎的經典 V12 法拉利絕對是我願望清單上的一項，我現在可以自豪地在清單旁邊打一個剔。再加上這輛車的前任車主 Harry Metcalfe 是我的 YouTube 頻道的一大靈感來源，這使得是次體驗更加美滿。

Production Years (for the GTS version only): 1972-1974
Engine: Carburetted 2.4 V6; 195HP
Total Production (for the GTS version only): 1,274 units

生產年份（僅限於 GTS 版本）：1972-1974
引擎：化油器 2.4 V6；195 匹馬力
總產量（僅限於 GTS 版本）：1,274 輛

Owner's remarks:

With beautiful looks and an intoxicating exhaust note, the Dino is my pride and joy, and the definite crown jewel of my collection.

車主的話：

Dino 外觀優美，排氣聲令人陶醉，它是我的喜樂，是我最引以為傲的珍藏。

Dino 246 GTS

(1973)

Anyone with an above-average level of Ferrari knowledge would know that the Dino GT was the first ever road car made by Ferrari that has the engine at the rear and with less than 12 cylinders. I have to say "the first car made by Ferrari" instead of "first Ferrari" because the Dino GT was never branded as a Ferrari, ever. It has always been said that the Dino GT was called the Dino (which is the name of Enzo's son who sadly died of illness back in 1956 at the young age of 24) because it was "not worthy" of the name Ferrari as the engine has less than 12 cylinders.

There is, however, a more emotional and beautiful background to the story. Dino was a passionate engineer at Ferrari before his untimely death. He was involved in the development of the V6 engine in Ferrari's Formula 2 racers. When the Dino road car was being developed some years later, and it was decided that it would house a V6 engine, Enzo decided to name the car Dino, in honour of his beloved son. Ferrari historians have said that there are letters at the time from Dino to Enzo about his V6 engine, saying that it was built as a "tribute" to his father's legendary 12-cylinder engines. So the actual story was hardly the cold "unworthy" version that popular media would have you believe.

The Dino 246 was produced from 1969-1974 and a lot more were made compared to its predecessor, the Dino 206. A total of 3,761 Dino 246's were made, of which only 1,274 were GTS' like the one we are reviewing here (the GTS version was only introduced in 1972). Unlike the aluminium Dino 206, the Dino 246 was made of steel to save cost. That means that they were prone to rust and many had major

對於法拉利有較深認識的人都知道，Dino GT 是法拉利生產的第一款後方中置引擎、且缸數少於 12 缸的公路車。我必須説是「法拉利生產的第一輛車」而不是「第一輛法拉利」，因為 Dino GT 從未被冠上法拉利的名號。據説 Dino GT 被稱為 Dino（Dino 是 Enzo 兒子的名字，不幸在 1956 年因病去世，享年 24 歲），是因為它的引擎缸數少於 12 缸，「不值得」配上法拉利之名。

其實，這個故事背後還有一個更悽美感人的背景。Dino 在他英年早逝之前是法拉利內一名充滿熱情的工程師。他參與了法拉利二級方程式賽車中 V6 引擎的開發。當法拉利幾年後開發 Dino GT 公路車型，並決定配上 V6 引擎時，Enzo 將車子命名為 Dino，以紀念他的愛子。研究法拉利的歷史學家表示，當時 Dino 寫給 Enzo 的信中提到他的 V6 引擎，稱其為對他父親傳奇的 12 缸引擎的「致敬」而製造的。因此，實際故事與流行媒體所描述的「不值得」版本完全不同。

Dino 246 的生產年份是 1969 年至 1974 年，與其前身 Dino 206 相比，生產數量多得多。車廠總共生產了 3,761 輛 Dino 246，其中只有 1,274 輛是這裏評測的 GTS 版本（GTS 版本於 1972 年才推出）。為了節省成本，Dino 246 是用鋼材製成的，而非 Dino 206 用鋁製，代表它們容易生鏽，而許多車輛在 1990 年代都有嚴重鏽蝕問題，因而價值較低。然而，此後價格飆升，許多車輛幸運地得到了修復。

當我坐進車內時，第一印象是這輛車看起來很小，但實際上並不感覺狹窄。內部就像你預期的那樣，一切都很精美並採用頂級材料製成。我喜歡該車廂內撥動掣的設計，它是法拉利從 Daytona 一直到 308 GTB/GTS 內飾中的同一設計。

當我啟動車子時，我注意到離合器不輕，但同時亦不是很重。我想應該可以輕鬆地應對交通擠塞。

rust issues when their values were low back in the 1990s. However, prices have since shot up and many examples have thankfully been restored since.

When inside the car, my first impression was that the car looked small but it actually did not feel cramped inside. The interior is as you would expect – everything is beautifully displayed and made with top grade materials. I love the toggle switches which were part of Ferrari interiors for a few generations from the Daytona all the way to the 308 GTB/GTS.

As I set off in the car I noticed the clutch was not light but certainly not heavy. I would imagine I can handle traffic jams in it easily. Everything else performed as I expected and I was happy to feel quite familiar in the car.

Finally, the climax of the drive was certainly the exhaust note. I have always known Dino's sound great but going through 1st to 5th gear in the driver's seat with the symphony at my back was a whole different experience! Despite "only" having 6 cylinders, the Dino always sounded more like its 12-cylinder siblings like the Daytona and BB 512 than the carburetted V8 308.

I have driven a lot of Ferrari's before, but the Dino was definitely the most intoxicating one to drive.

除此之外，其他的運作都跟我的預期一樣，這輛車令我感到非常熟悉。

最後，試車的高潮無疑是排氣聲音。我一向知道 Dino 的聲音很棒，但在駕駛席上從一波轉到五波的過程，伴隨着引擎的交響樂，是完全不同的體驗！儘管「僅有」6 缸，但 Dino 的聲音總是更像其他 12 氣缸車系，比如 Daytona 和 BB 512，而非化油器 V8 引擎的 308。

我開過很多法拉利，但 Dino 絕對是其中令人最陶醉的一輛。

Production Years (for the carburetted version only): 1975-1980
Engine: Carburetted 3.0 V8; 255HP
Total Production (for the carburetted GTB version only): 2,897 units

生產年份（僅限於化油器版本）：1975-1980
引擎：化油器 3.0 V8；255 匹馬力
總產量（僅限於化油器 GTB 版本）：2,897 輛

Owner's remarks:

Some forty years ago, I bought my first supercar. It was a Ferrari 308 GTB, and from there on, I began my Ferrari ownership journey.

Unlike today, supercar owners then rarely took their supercars out. Most supercars were kept in the carport. Taking a Ferrari onto the street in those days was a very unique experience, most people were not able to tell what car it was. Heads turned, people stopped in front of traffic lights to take a deeper look at it, some even came over to ask about the car.

255 HP in the 1980s was colossal. The sheer engine power made you invincible in front of traffic lights. Mid-engine, four Weber carburettors, pop-up headlights, manual dog leg gated shift, pure mechanical with no electronic aid, unique Ferrari scent of the all-round leather interior and upholstery, I had an unparalleled driving experience behind the steering wheel.

車主的話：

大約 40 年前，我購入了第一輛超跑。那是法拉利 308 GTB，從那時起，展開了我的法拉利車主之旅。

與今天不同，當時的超跑車主很少駕着他們的超跑出門。大多數超跑都被安置在車房裏。那時在街上開法拉利是一種非常獨特的體驗，大多數人都無法辨認出這是甚麼車。人們紛紛轉過頭來，或在紅綠燈前停下來仔細觀察，甚至有人過來詢問這輛車的情況。

在 1980 年代，255 匹馬力是巨大的。強大的引擎動力使你在交通燈前立於不敗之地。中置引擎，四個 Weber 化油器，自動翻出的車頭大燈，手動 dog leg 格式檔閘轉波，純機械結構，沒有電子輔助，獨特的法拉利全皮內飾令全車瀰漫着皮飾氣味，給予我無與倫比的駕駛體驗。

Ferrari 法拉利
308 GTB (1981)

Whenever people talk about "1980s poster cars", naturally they refer to the Lamborghini Countach and Ferrari Testarossa. However, one very iconic 1980s car that is often forgotten in this context is the Ferrari 308. The first contemporary "entry model" by Ferrari during the flamboyant 1980s made the 308 popular both on the streets and on the big screen. Just like the Testarossa with *Miami Vice*, the 308 too, had its own popular police TV show, *Magnum P.I.*.

As the first official "baby" Ferrari, the 308 was an instant success. It had a long production run from 1975 to 1985 and was for the longest time Ferrari's bestselling model with 12,000 units made – a record only beaten relatively recently by the 360 Modena (16,000+ units made).

All early 308's had a carburetted 2-valve-per-cylinder V8 engine which produced 255HP. In 1980, however, Ferrari had to switch to fuel injected engines due to emission regulation changes. This decreased the power to a mere 211HP and an even more pathetic 203HP for US cars (due to even tighter emission controls in the US) Ferrari rectified this problem swiftly and introduced the quattrovalvole version in 1982, where the fuel injected 308 V8 engines were improved by having 4-valves-per-cylinder. Power output was increased back to 235HP, which was still less than the early carburetted engines. While the carburetted engine is prone to more mood swings and requires regular tuning of its carburettors (especially during season/weather changes), it is widely recognised today as the most raw and pure engine to have, in addition to being the most powerful.

每當人們談論「1980 年代的海報汽車」，自然會提到林寶堅尼 Countach 和法拉利 Testarossa。然而在這個時期，卻有一輛非常具標誌性的 80 年代汽車經常被人遺忘，那就是法拉利 308。作為在華麗的 1980 年代法拉利所推出的第一款「入門車型」，308 在街上和大熒幕上都廣受歡迎。就像 Testarossa 在電影《邁阿密風雲》中一樣，308 也有自己受歡迎的警察電視節目《神探猛龍》。

作為第一輛官方的「小型號」法拉利，308 立即獲得了成功。它的生產週期從 1975 年至 1985 年，長達 10 年，一直是法拉利最暢銷的車型，共生產了 12,000 輛——這個紀錄直到最近才被 360 Modena（生產了超過 16,000 輛）打破。

所有早期的 308 都安裝了化油器，每缸兩氣門 V8 引擎，可產生 255 匹馬力。然而，由於 1980 年修訂排放法規，法拉利不得不轉為使用燃油噴注引擎。這將功率降低至僅有 211 匹馬力，美國版本更只有 203 匹馬力（美國的排放管制更為嚴格）。法拉利迅速糾正了這個問題，於 1982 年推出了四氣門引擎版本。動力輸出回升至 235 匹馬力，但仍比早期的化油器引擎少。儘管化油器引擎的表現不穩定，需要定期調校（特別是在季節／天氣變化時），但今天人們廣泛認為它是最原始、最純粹，而且最強大的 308 引擎。

坐在車裏，立刻感覺到相當擠迫！頂部空間極小，車廂感覺狹窄。我無法想像身高超過 6 英尺的人會如何應付。不過，這種潛在的幽閉感很快就會被那些華麗的黑底橙字的 Veglia Borletti 儀表盤和撥動桿分散了注意。啟動引擎的程序與 Dino 246 相似，你要將油門踩下三分之二，轉動鑰匙，引擎啟動後立即釋放油門。

雖然 308 處於我們曾評測過的 Dino 246 GTS（見

First immediate impression once seated in the car is that it is quite cramped! Headspace is minimal and the cabin feels narrow. I cannot imagine how a 6ft+ person would manage. However, any potential claustrophobic feeling would quickly be distracted by those beautiful orange-on-black Veglia Borletti dials and toggle switches. The engine start procedure is similar to the Dino 246, where you press the throttle about 2/3 down, turn the keys and release the throttle the moment the engine fires up.

While the 308 pretty much sits right between the Dino 246 GTS we reviewed (see page 48) and my own 328 GTS, its engine sounds like neither. Compared to its younger and older siblings, its engine sounds a lot more barky. I think Harry Metcalfe of Harry's Garage (YouTube channel) was spot on when he said the 308 sounded more like the Ford Escort 4-cylinder rally cars of the era than a V8. Still, it sounds good and potent.

The engine feels and pulls strong. It may not be faster than my 328, but the way the carburetted engine pulls and sounds makes the whole experience feel faster and more raw. Everything else is as you would expect. The steering is heavy when the car is slow as there is no power steering, the gear changes are not too different from both the Dino or my 328, and everything is positioned similarly. The clutch is a little bit heavier than both the Dino and the 328, but still comfortable.

All in all, I was impressed with the 308 GTB, which is hardly surprising. The drive feels more raw and pure than my 328, and since its exterior design gives a nod to the BB512, one of my dream cars, I will pick the looks of the 308 over my 328 every day of the week.

第 48 頁）和我的 328 GTS 之間，但它的引擎聲音卻與兩者都不同。與它年幼和年長的同系車相比，308 的引擎聲音更接近吠哮聲。我認為 Harry Metcalfe 的 Harry's Garage（YouTube 頻道）對此的評價很準確。他說 308 的聲音更像是當時的福特 Escort 四氣缸拉力車，而不是 V8 引擎。不過，它聽起來很棒，並且充滿力量。

引擎感覺強勁，並有很好的動力。它可能不比我的 328 快，但化油器引擎的拉力和聲音使整個駕駛體驗感覺上更快、更純粹。其他一切都一如預期。當車子緩慢行駛時，方向盤很沉重，因為沒有風油軚；轉波與 Dino 或我的 328 沒有太大的不同，一切的排列都相似。離合器比 Dino 和 328 重一點，但仍然很舒適。

總括而言，我對 308 GTB 印象深刻，這一點是毋庸置疑的。駕駛感覺比我的 328 更原始和純粹，由於其外觀設計是向我其中一輛夢寐以求的汽車 BB512 作出致敬，所以我會選擇 308 的外觀，而不選 328。

Production Years: 1985-1989
Engine: Fuel injected 3.2 V8; 270HP
Total Production (for the GTS version only): 6,068 units

生產年份：1985-1989
引擎：燃油噴注 3.2 V8；270 匹馬力
總產量（僅限於 GTS 版本）：6,068 輛

Owner's remarks:

Growing up in the 1980s and 1990s, I have always been obsessed with Ferrari's of that era. Flagship models like the BB512 and Testarossa are too cost-prohibitive to own with their sky-high maintenance costs. The 328 is therefore the perfect balance – similar looks but with very reasonable maintenance needs. The fact that it is a very analogue car means it is similarly engaging to drive.

車主的話：

在 20 世紀 80 年代和 90 年代成長的我，一直對當時的法拉利着迷。旗艦型號像 BB512 和 Testarossa 因維修成本高昂而令人卻步。328 因此成為完美的平衡──外觀相似，但維修需求非常合理。它是一輛非常相類的車，可以帶來同樣的駕駛樂趣。

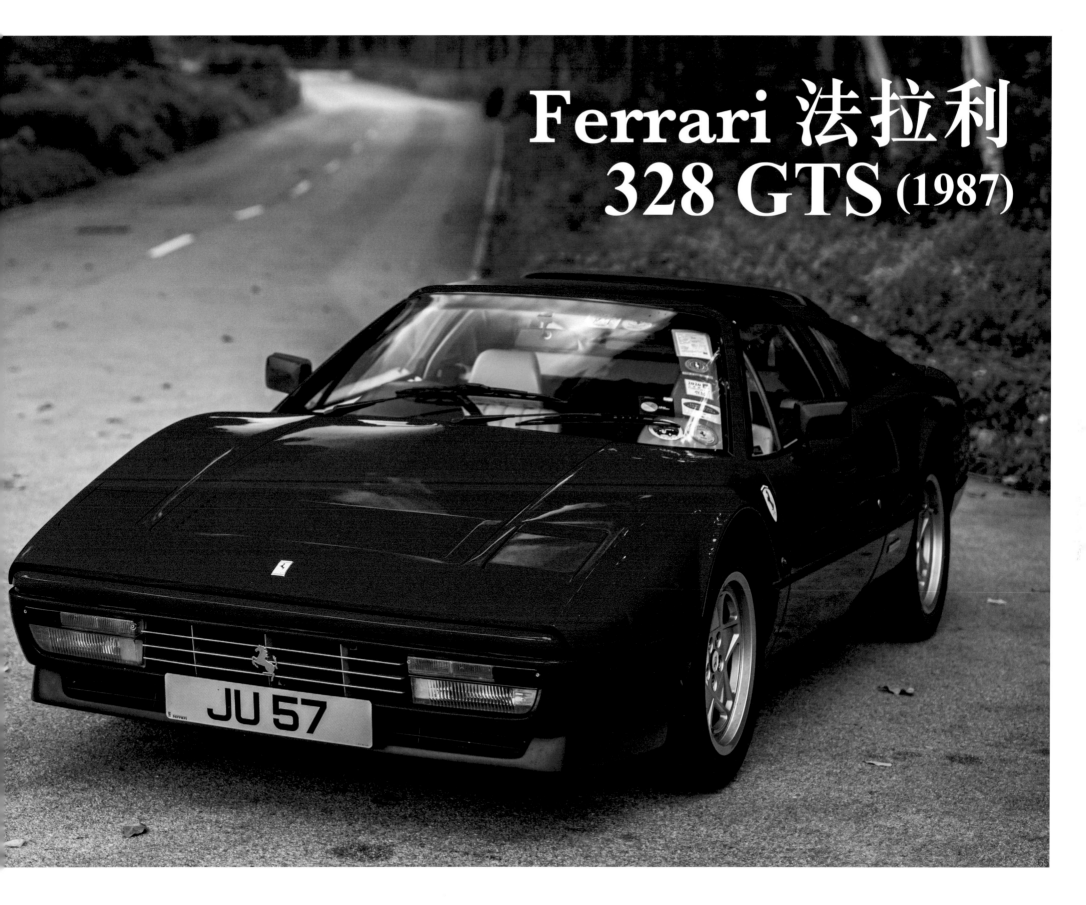

Ferrari 法拉利
328 GTS (1987)

This review is particularly special because it is a review of my very own 1987 Ferrari 328 GTS. Those of you familiar with Ferrari would know that the 328 was the successor of the hugely successful 308. The 308 was Ferrari's first official mid-engine Ferrari (the 206 / 246 and 308 GT4 Dino's were, well, Dino's and not Ferrari) and it was an instant hit. Throughout the 308's production run from 1975 to 1985, Ferrari made more than 12,000 308's, outnumbering any previous models by far.

Hence when it was time to release the new 328 model, Ferrari did not make too many changes to the 308's winning formula. The most visible changes were the headlights – which were replaced by bigger, rectangular lenses imbedded into the front bumper – aligning with the Testarossa's design. Both the 308 and 328 were designed by Pininfarina's Leonardo Fioravanti – a talented and predominant figure who designed some of Ferrari's most iconic models, including the Dino 206 / 246, Daytona, BB512, Testarossa, 288 GTO and F40.

The 328's production run was shorter than the 308; going from only 1985 to 1989. During this time, 7,412 328's were made, with the GTS version outnumbering the GTB version with a 5 to 1 ratio. 6,068 GTS' were made compared to only 1,344 GTB's; as a result, the GTB is the more desirable pick today due to rarity.

The 328 uses the 308 series' final engine – the V8 quattrovalve (or quattrovalvole in Italian) engine – but the capacity was increased from 3.0 litres to 3.2 litres – hence the designation "328" (3.2 litre V8). Power was also increased from the 308 QV's 235HP to now 270HP.

這篇評測非常特別，因為對象是我的 1987 年法拉利 328 GTS。對熟悉法拉利的人來說，328 是極其成功的 308 後繼車型。308 是第一款正式中置引擎的法拉利車型（206/246 和 308 GT4 Dino 是 Dino 車型而不是法拉利），並且一炮而紅。在 308 於 1975 年至 1985 年的生產過程中，法拉利生產了超過 12,000 輛 308，數量遠遠超過以前的任何車型。

因此，當法拉利發佈新的 328 型號時，仍依據 308 的成功方程式，沒有太大更改。最明顯的變化是大燈，用上更大的矩形鏡片，鑲嵌在前保險槓中，與 Testarossa 的設計吻合。308 和 328 都由 Pininfarina 的 Leonardo Fioravanti 設計，他是一位才華橫溢的顯赫人物，設計了不少法拉利最具代表性的車型，包括 Dino 206/246、Daytona、BB512、Testarossa、288 GTO 和 F40。

328 的生產週期比 308 短，只有 1985 年至 1989 年這幾年。在這段時間內，車廠生產了 7,412 輛 328，其中 GTS 版本以 5 比 1 的比例超過 GTB 版本。車廠生產了 6,068 輛 GTS，而 GTB 僅有 1,344 輛。GTB 因其稀有性更受人追捧。

328 使用了 308 系列的最終引擎——V8 四氣門引擎，但排汽量從 3.0 公升增加到 3.2 公升——因此被命名為「328」（3.2 公升 V8）。功率也從 308 QV 的 235 匹馬力增加到現在的 270 匹馬力。

直到今天，我對能如此輕鬆地駕駛 328 感到驚訝和難忘。離合器不重，咬合點易於掌握，離合器行程很大。坐椅也很合適，沒有「手長腳短」的問題，這在一般（或者說是刻板印象中）的舊式意大利汽車中很常見。然而，位於一側的 fly-off 手掣離我有點太遠，有時在斜坡上忽忙起步時有機會拉傷肌肉。情感上，感受帶有獨特「叮噹聲」的外露式檔閘波棍，並握着那個簡單但具有代表性的法拉利方向盤，令人感到夢想成真。

I remain surprised and impressed to this day by how easy it is to drive the 328. The clutch is not heavy, and the biting point is easy to manage with generous clutch travel. The seating position also fits me well, with no "long arms, short legs" issue as typically (or rather, stereotypically) found in older Italian cars. The fly-off hand brake on the side, however, is a bit too far up front and there have been occasions when I pulled a muscle reaching for it when rushing off traffic lights on a slope. Emotionally, going through the open gated shifter with that distinctive "clink" and holding that simple but iconic Ferrari steering wheel is a dream come true.

I grew up during the 1980s and 1990s and Hong Kong was a very different place then. To see a Ferrari was a rare occasion. I would count my lucky stars if I saw more than one on the road in a month. The looks, touch, and smell of an 80s/90s Ferrari never fail to bring back those childhood memories. Candidly, I would have preferred the BB512 or Testarossa for their jaw-dropping looks. However, the maintenance issues of those, being a few cylinders more, and an engine-out required for every cambelt change thanks to the engine being longitudinally-mounted, is just too much for me. The usability of flat 12 Ferrari's in Hong Kong is also limited. As such, I have happily "settled" for this 328 since I can take it out anytime I want, the only consideration being the weather. For these reasons, I highly recommend the 328 for anybody who wants to try a classic/modern classic Ferrari.

我在 1980 至 1990 年代成長，當時香港是一個與別不同的地方。法拉利十分罕見。如果我在一個月內遇到超過一輛法拉利在路上行駛，我會覺得非常幸運。1980 至 1990 年代法拉利的外觀、觸感和氣味總能令人喚起童年回憶。坦白說，我寧願擁有 BB512 或 Testarossa，因為它們的外觀令人驚嘆。然而，那些汽車的維修問題，源於多出來的幾個汽缸，以及每次更換引擎正時皮帶都需要取出引擎（因為引擎是縱向放置的），對我來說太過繁瑣。何況在香港，12 缸汽車也無用武之地。因此，我很高興並「滿足於」這輛 328，因為我可以隨時開它出去，唯一需要考慮的就是天氣。基於這些原因，我向任何想要體驗老爺 / 現代經典法拉利汽車的人強烈推薦 328。

Production Years: 1989-1995
Engine: Fuel injected 3.4 V8; 320HP
Total Production (for the facelifted GTB version only): 252 units

生產年份：1989-1995
引擎：燃油噴注 3.4 V8；320 匹馬力
總產量（僅限於翻新 GTB 版本）：252 輛

Owner's remarks:

348GTB

Modern Classic

Beautiful, especially the pop-up lights and door sides details

Enjoy the rev above 4000RPM

The non-power steering and clutch are good physical exercise

車主的話：

348GTB

現代經典

華麗，尤其是彈出的車頭燈和門側細節

享受 4,000 轉以上的轉速

欠缺風油軚以及沉重的離合器都是很好的鍛煉

Ferrari 法拉利
348 GTB (1994)

As you may have figured out by now, we at InstacarHK are huge fans of the classic Ferrari V8 line up, and we are proud to finally track down the elusive 348 GTB. Elusive not because they made very few of them, quite the contrary in fact, as Ferrari made a total of 8,844 348's in different variants. But elusive because, and there is no polite way to say this, they have always been unpopular.

The earliest models (known as the 348 TB and 348 TS for the hardtop and targa versions, respectively) were allegedly not very good to drive. They were heavy, slow, and had unpredictable handling. *Car* magazine's Richard Bremner revealed in an issue of *Enzo* magazine that back in 1989 when he was at Fiorano for the 348's media launch event, even legendary Ferrari test driver Dario Benuzzi lost control at the very first corner when giving Richard a media ride.

The 348 we are reviewing here is the "facelift" version, the GTB, which Ferrari introduced in 1993 in order to address the aforementioned shortcomings of the earlier models. The facelift versions were improved with an increased power output, from the earlier version's 300HP to 320HP, thanks to an enhanced engine management system and a new exhaust system. The suspension setup was revised and the rear track was also widened by one inch in order to address the handling issues. Of the 8,844 348's Ferrari made from 1989-1995, only 252 are the GTB's (and 137 GTS models), making this a very rare car especially in RHD.

Getting into the car, the first thing I noticed was how solid and refined it is compared to my 328 GTS.

相信讀者可能已經猜到，我們 InstacarHK 都是經典法拉利 V8 系列的忠實粉絲，而且我們很自豪最終找到了難以捉摸的 348 GTB。說難以捉摸並不是因為這款車的產量太少，事實上恰恰相反，法拉利總共生產了 8,844 輛不同型號的 348。但之所以難以捉摸，坦白講，是因為它們一直不受歡迎。

最早的車型（稱為 348 TB 和 348 TS，分別指硬頂和敞篷版本）據稱駕駛體驗並不好。它們又重又慢，而且操控不穩。《汽車》雜誌的 Richard Bremner 在《Enzo》雜誌的一期中透露，1989 年他參加 348 在意大利費奧拉諾的媒體發佈會時，即使是傳奇法拉利試車手 Dario Benuzzi 在給 Richard 提供媒體試車時，也在第一個彎道失控。

在這裏評測的這輛 348，是法拉利於 1993 年推出的「翻新」版本——GTB，它旨在解決早期車型上述的問題。經過翻新後，由於引入引擎管理系統和新的排氣系統，翻新版本的動力輸出從早期版本的 300 匹馬力增加到 320 匹馬力。這個版本修訂了避震設定，後軌距離增加了 1 英寸，解決了操控的問題。在 1989 年至 1995 年期間，法拉利共生產了 8,844 輛 348，其中僅有 252 輛是 GTB 型號（還有 137 輛 GTS 型號），因而成為一款非常罕見的車，特別是右軚版。

進入車內，我首先注意到，與我的 328 GTS 相比，它是多麼堅固和精緻。整個內部感覺很舒適，造工也很精良。進入 dog leg 格式波箱的一波，轉波操作也更精細，感覺轉波像是經過彈簧輔助，相比之下，328 的轉波需要更大力量。離合器有一定的重量，但不影響使用。啟動汽車後，感覺更像豪華巡航跑車型號，而不是 328。這輛車裝有 Capristo 排氣管，聲音聽起來很棒，車主告訴我原裝排氣聽起來相當溫和。車內環境和排氣聲音實際上更接近 360 Modena，而不是 328，令人十分驚訝。但也許

The entire interior feels a lot more comfortable and well-made. Slotting into the dog leg first gear, even the gear change is more refined, with what feels like a spring-assisted gear selection compared to the sheer force needed in the 328. The clutch has weight to it but nothing obstructive. Setting off, the car feels more GT-like than the 328. This car has the Capristo exhaust which sounds superb, as the owner told me the original exhaust was rather tame. The ambience of the interior and the exhaust note are actually closer to the 360 Modena than the 328, which I was surprised by. But perhaps I should not be, because the 328 was largely based on the 308, which was developed in the mid-1970s and therefore the 308 / 328 line should indeed feel like a dinosaur when compared to the 348.

Performance-wise, the car does feel heavy and not particularly fast. In fact, one thing that does feel closer to the 328 is the 348's straight line speed. It did not feel particularly quicker than the 328, although it gets up to speed in a more comfortable fashion, due to the increased torque, whereas the 328 gets to similar speeds more dramatically.

All in all, I can understand why the 348 was criticised when it was released. Its performance and speed are a little underwhelming. This is especially true when its German and Japanese rivals were already making some pretty quick cars in the 1990s. However, like many classics, this no longer matters as you buy a classic like this today to enjoy its analogue feel, its simple technology from yesteryears, and history. You certainly do not buy one for the sheer speed. I have therefore genuinely enjoyed my drive in the 348 GTB.

我不應該有這種感覺,因為 328 是依據 308 開發的,而 308 在 20 世紀 70 年代開發,因此與 348 相比,308/328 系列感覺有點老。

在性能方面,這輛車感覺很重,而且速度不是特別快。實際上,與 328 更接近的是其直線速度。雖然 348 的扭力增加,能以更舒適的形式達到相似的速度,但似乎沒有比 328 快多少,而 328 則能更顯著地加速。

總括而言,我能理解為甚麼 348 在推出時備受批評。它的性能和速度有些令人失望。特別是當德國和日本的競爭對手在 1990 年代已經生產出一些相當快的汽車時。然而,就像許多老爺車一樣,這已經不再重要,因為你購買這樣的老爺車是為了享受與之相關的感覺,以及它的簡單技術和歷史。你肯定不是為了速度而購買它的。因此,我真正享受駕駛 348 GTB 的樂趣。

Production Years: 1994-1999
Engine: Fuel injected 3.5 V8; 375HP
Total Production (for the F1 Berlinetta version only): 1,042 units

生產年份：1994-1999
引擎：燃油噴注 3.5 V8；375 匹馬力
總產量（僅限於 F1 Berlinetta 版本）：1,042 輛

Owner's remarks:

My ownership of the Ferrari F355 was sparked by my admiration of the F1 gear shifting mechanism, which was one of the latest technologies adopted by Ferrari at the time. In my opinion, the F1-style paddle gear shift is one of the most underrated features among all of Ferrari's forefront innovations. The Ferrari F355 Berlinetta F1 model is the first road car ever to be equipped with the gearbox derived directly from Formula 1. It has paved the way for future gear shifting mechanisms, dominating most car models in the industry today.

車主的話：

我擁有法拉利 F355 是因為我對其一級方程式轉波機制的崇拜，這是當時法拉利採用的最新技術之一。我認為，一級方程式格式的撥片轉波是法拉利所有前沿創新中最被低估的功能之一。法拉利 F355 Berlinetta F1 型號是第一輛直接安裝來自一級方程式波箱的公路車。它為未來的轉波機制開拓了一片天，並在今天主導了行業中大多數汽車型號。

Ferrari 法拉利
355 F1 Berlinetta (1997)

The F355 was globally captivating when it was released. In Hollywood, no one can forget Nicholas Cage progressively destroying one in a car chase with Sean Connery in a Hummer H1 through the streets of San Francisco in *The Rock*. For the much younger crowd, there was the "more than you can afford, pal" black F355 Spider in the original *Fast & Furious* that lost a drag race to Paul Walker's Supra. And who can forget the F355 GTS in James Bond's *Goldeneye*?

Of course, when Ferrari released the F355 in 1995, it wasn't just about the good looks. Ferrari had to make something extra special after the (sometimes unfair) negative reviews of the preceding 348. As such, the power unit was increased to 3.5 litre and most importantly, for the first time in the V8 line up, Ferrari went from 4-valves per cylinder to 5-valves per cylinder; hence the model designation 355 (3.5 litre and 5-valves). Lighter pistons and crank not only increased its power from the 348's 320HP to 375HP, but also allowed the engine to rev to 8,500RPM for the first time, thereby starting the high-revving distinct character of V8 Ferrari's. Significantly, the F355 was the first ever car where Ferrari introduced its F1 transmission – a technology directly derived from its Formula 1 race cars as the name suggests.

The car in review is a F1 Berlinetta (i.e. hardtop coupe). I was actually rather excited to try an F1 version instead of the manual, as I have always wondered how the first ever generation F1 transmission was like. Sitting in the car, it doesn't feel too different from the 348 GTB we reviewed previously, both are clearly cars from the 1990s.

F355 一推出就引起了全球的關注。在荷李活，沒有人會忘記在電影《石破天驚》中，Nicholas Cage 駕駛着破爛的 F355，與 Sean Connery 駕駛的軍用悍馬 H1 在舊金山街頭，展開一場汽車追逐戰。對於年輕觀眾來説，電影《狂野時速》中，有一輛「超出你所能負擔的」黑色 F355 Spider，在一場直路賽中輸給了 Paul Walker 的 Supra。還有，誰會忘記占士邦在電影《黃金眼》中駕駛 F355 GTS 的場景？

當然，當法拉利在 1995 年推出 F355 時，不僅僅是因為外型美觀。在此之前的 348 受到了（有時不公平的）負面評價後，法拉利必須生產一些特別亮眼的車型。因此，法拉利將 355 的動力裝置增加到 3.5 公升，而最重要的是，首次在 V8 車型中，從每缸四個氣門增加到五個氣門；這便是 355（3.5 公升和 5 個氣門）名字的由來。更輕的活塞和曲軸不僅將其功率從 348 的 320 匹馬力增加到 375 匹馬力，而且還首次使引擎的轉速達到每分鐘 8,500 轉，由此開始了法拉利 V8 高轉速的獨特性格。值得注意的是，F355 是第一輛採用法拉利一級方程式波箱的汽車，顧名思義，這項技術直接源自其一級方程式賽車。

這次評測的汽車是 F1 Berlinetta（即硬頂轎跑車）。我很高興試駕的是一級方程式版本而非棍波版本，因為我一直想知道第一代一級方程式波箱是怎樣的。坐在車裏，它與之前評測的 348 GTB 並沒有太大的不同，兩者顯然都是來自 1990 年代的車。

當我在空曠的地方踩上油門，每分鐘 8,500 轉的紅線確實與早期型號有所不同，引擎第一次唱起歌來。在油門全開時，引擎聲音令人陶醉——許多人認為 F355 在整個法拉利 V8 車型中擁有最佳的排氣聲音，我也認同這一點。然而，即使以 1990 年代的標準來説，汽車的速度也不特別令人印象深刻。

Out in the open and stepping on it, the 8,500RPM redline really distinguishes itself from earlier models. The engine, for the first time, sings. When on full throttle, the engine note is truly intoxicating – many have commented that the F355 has the best exhaust note out of the entire Ferrari V8 line up, and I tend to agree with that. However, the speed of the car is not particularly impressive, even for 1990s standard. Even though the engine sings beautifully, it does not feel particularly fast or dramatically faster than the 348 GTB. The 360 Modena and F430 that came after are clearly in an entirely different league.

On the F1 transmission, while as expected the gear shift times are slower than the models that came after it, it still shifts reasonably quickly. It does not feel like an unsophisticated system when on the move. However, you can feel its primitive technology when in less straightforward situations, such as entering roundabouts, where the driver may not be fully determined to stop or to set off. That is when the clutch hesitates and could not decide whether it wants to engage or disengage, causing delays and knocks. In that sense, I am not sure the 355 F1 can be as good a daily driver as its manual counterpart.

Regardless, none of these really matter, as buyers of the 355 today are not buying the car for its straight line speed or gear shift times, but for the nostalgic feeling that the car inspires and its timeless design.

儘管引擎聲音美麗動人，但感覺並不特別快或比 348 GTB 快很多。與之後推出的 360 Modena 和 F430 相比，明顯處於完全不同的水平。

至於一級方程式波箱，一如預期，轉波時間比之後的車型慢，但它在行駛時的轉波速度仍然合理地快，而非原始的系統。然而，在較為複雜的情況下，例如進入迴旋處，當駕駛者可能無法完全確定停下還是啟動時，會感覺到它的原始技術，此時離合器會顯得猶豫，無法決定是否應該啟動或脫離，導致延遲和顛簸。在這方面，我不確定 355 一級方程式版能否像棍波版一樣適合日常駕駛。

不過，這些都非真正要緊的事情，因為如今 F355 的買家不是為了它的直線速度或轉波時間而購買此車，倒是為了懷舊感和其永恆的設計。

Production Years: 1991-1994
Engine: Fuel injected 5.0 flat-12; 430HP
Total Production: 2,261 units

生產年份：1991-1994
引擎：燃油噴注 5.0 水平對向 12 缸引擎；430 匹馬力
總產量：2,261 輛

Owner's remarks:

The only time I have ever driven up to 300KM/HR was in a Ferrari 512 TR many years ago (abroad, of course!). Since then, I have always wanted to own one, and when the opportunity arose, I immediately bought one. I no longer drive at 300KM/HR now, but the car is still extremely enjoyable.

車主的話：

我唯一一次以每小時 300 公里的速度駕駛，是多年前駕駛着一輛法拉利 512 TR 時（當然是在國外！）。從那時起，我一直想擁有一輛法拉利 512 TR，而當時機一到，我毫不猶豫買下了它。雖然我現在不再以每小時 300 公里的速度駕駛，但這輛車仍然非常令人神往。

Ferrari 法拉利
512 TR (1994)

The Ferrari 512 TR belongs to the legendary Testarossa line up that conquered the 1980s. Everybody would have heard of the hit TV show *Miami Vice*, where Don Johnson portrays an undercover cop drifting around Miami in a beautiful white Testarossa in pursuit of Miami drug lords. The 512 TR is the second iteration of the Testarossa line up, still retaining the 5 litre flat-12 engine from the Testarossa, but with various upgrades including a new transmission system, a new intake system, a new exhaust system, and a new Bosch engine management system. As a result, the 512 TR produced 430HP, a significant increase over the original Testarossa's 390HP.

When inside the car, it immediately feels a lot roomier than its younger V8 siblings, like my very own 328 GTS. Other than that, much of the interior feels and smells like any other Ferrari's of its era. As for the clutch, it is noticeably heavier than its V8 counterparts. That said, it is not cumbersome and remains easy to drive and engage. However, I can imagine it would be quite challenging and tiring if you are stuck in a traffic jam in a 512 TR.

Other than the clutch, everything else felt familiar to me, from the black dials with orange fonts to the dog leg five-speed gearbox and the fly-off handbrake. One thing, however, that none of the V8 Ferrari's I have ever owned or driven could compare with, is the engine. The 12-cylinder engine in the 512 TR reminds you that it is something special the moment you turn the key. From the moment of that initial roar, I knew this was going to be a life-changing test drive. And life-changing it was.

I have sat in Testarossa's and BB 512's many

法拉利 512 TR 屬於風靡 1980 年代的傳奇 Testarossa 車型。每個人都聽說過《邁阿密風暴》這部熱門電視劇,當中 Don Johnson 飾演一名臥底警探,在邁阿密的街道上駕駛着一輛漂亮的白色 Testarossa 追捕毒品頭目。512 TR 是 Testarossa 車型的第二代,仍然保留着 Testarossa 的 5 公升水平對向 12 缸引擎,只是進行了各種升級,包括新的波箱系統、新的進氣系統、新的排氣系統和新的 Bosch 引擎管理系統。因此,512 TR 的功率達到了 430 匹馬力,比原始 Testarossa 的 390 匹馬力增加不少。

坐在車內,立刻感覺車廂比我的 328 GTS 的 V8 車系更寬敞。除此之外,車廂內的大部份感覺和氣味都與同年代的法拉利相似。至於離合器,明顯比 V8 車系的車要重。儘管如此,它並不笨重,仍然容易駕駛和啟動。但是,可以想像如果開着 512 TR 遇到堵車,將是相當具挑戰性和令人疲累的事。

除了離合器,其他一切對我來說都很熟悉,從黑色表盤上的橙色字體到 dog leg 格式五速波箱和 fly-off 手掣。無論如何,任何一輛我曾經擁有或駕駛過的 V8 法拉利引擎都無法與之相比。512 TR 的 12 缸引擎在你轉動鑰匙的那一刻,就會提醒你它的獨特之處。從那一刻的初始咆哮,我知道這將是一次改變生命的試車。而它確實改變了我的生命。

我以前曾多次坐進 Testarossa 和 BB 512 上,我知道它們的聲音是怎樣的,但是用我的右腳和左腳穿梭於轉波之間來指揮引擎交響樂卻是另一回事。引擎的聲音如此令人陶醉,以至於有時你不會意識到,以今天的標準來說,它輸出的 430 匹馬力實際上並不算快。對於這輛車因太寬闊而備受當年人們的批評,可以完全拋到九霄雲外。相比今天的標準,這輛車一點也不寬闊。

在我對 Murciélago 的評測中(見第 120 頁),我對它過份舒適和寧靜的豪華巡航跑車定位抱怨不

times before so I know how they sound like, but to be conducting the engine symphony with my right and left foot as I run through the gears is truly something else. The engine sound is so intoxicating that for a while you fail to realise that for today's standard, the 430HP it pumps out is actually not that fast. The period criticism that this car received for being too wide can be thrown out the window in its entirety. The car is not big at all for today's standard.

In my Murciélago review (see page 120), I bemoaned it for being too comfortable and muted of a grand tourer that it really did not fit its aggressive looks. Fortunately, this was not the case for the 512 TR. The 512 TR is so different in the sensation that it provides. The gear shifts, the steering, and of course, the exhaust note, trigger all your senses every time you step on it – everything feels 10 times more captivating than the much newer Murciélago.

To be clear, I do not believe the reason for this is because the 512 TR is necessarily a better car than the Murciélago, but more that the 512 TR is an older car compared to the Murciélago. The 512 TR is from an era where gas pedals, clutch pedals, gear shifts, and cabin sound deadening were all less sophisticated and less comfort-oriented than the era of the Murciélago. Therefore, even though the 512 TR is also a grand tourer, it provides a much better driving experience than the Murciélago.

It has been such a pleasure to review one of my favourite Ferrari models – a major bucket list item checked. They say never meet your heroes, well they were wrong in this case.

已，實際上這並不配合其激進的外觀。幸好 512 TR 給人的感覺完全不同。不論轉波、轉向，還有排氣聲音，每次踩油門時都會觸發你所有的感官——一切都比新得多的 Murciélago 吸引十倍。

需要說明一點，我不認為 512 TR 必然比 Murciélago 更好，而只是因為 512 TR 比 Murciélago 更老舊。與 Murciélago 相比，512 TR 所處的時代不論油門踏板、離合器踏板、波桿和駕駛室隔音功能都比較落後，也不太注重舒適度。因此，即使 512 TR 也是一款豪華巡航跑車，但它的駕駛體驗反而比 Murciélago 更好，更有感覺。

能夠評測我最喜歡的其中一款法拉利車型，真是一大樂事，我完成了願望清單上的一個重要項目。人們總說永遠不要與你的英雄見面，但在這種情況下，他們大錯特錯。

Production Years: 1996-2001
Engine: Fuel injected 5.5 V12; 485HP
Total Production: 3,083 units

生產年份：1996-2001
引擎：燃油噴注 5.5 V12；485 匹馬力
總產量：3,083 輛

Owner's remarks:

There is something magical to a Ferrari V12 which most boys dream of growing up. When I sold my 355 some 20 years ago, I was considering which Ferrari to buy next. The decision boiled down to a 550 manual or a 575 F1. Considering the 550 maybe the last of the famous gated Ferrari, I decided to go for her.

During my 20 years of ownership, the 550 has gone through substantial restoration and was one of the earliest cars to obtain the Ferrari Classiche certificate from Blackbird Ferrari Hong Kong. My plan is to pass the car to the next generation as the pride and joy of the family!

車主的話：

對於大多數男孩子來說，法拉利的 V12 引擎總是充滿着神奇的魔力。大約 20 年前，當我賣掉自己的 355 之後，我開始考慮下一輛要買哪款法拉利。我最終的選擇落到 550 棍波版或 575 F1 版。考慮到 550 可能是最後一輛擁有著名手動轉波系統的法拉利，於是我決定選擇它。

在我擁有這輛 550 的 20 年裏，經過大量修復，它成為了最早獲得 Blackbird Ferrari Hong Kong 頒發 Ferrari Classiche 證書的汽車之一。我計劃將這輛車傳承給下一代，成為家族的驕傲和喜悦！

Ferrari 法拉利
550 Maranello (1997)

I have never been a fan of former Ferrari President Luca di Montezemolo's decision to revert back to a front-engine layout for Ferrari's flagship 12-cylinder models. After 23 years of aesthetic perfection with the mid-engined Berlinetta Boxer and Testarossa, in 1996, the front-engined 550 Maranello was released.

Luca di Montezemolo was determined to make their flagship model more useable and comfortable, something which the front-engine layout was able to offer. With the engine at the front and separated from the transmission at the back, the engine's centre of gravity is lower, and the overall front and rear weight distribution is also better balanced. More importantly, with a conventional rear boot, luggage and the all-important golf bags can fit in the boot nicely for cross continent road trips (as this car was designed as a grand tourer). Ferrari produced the manual-only 550 Maranello from 1996 to 2001 and built a total of 3,083 units, making it a proper rare car for today's standards.

The engine in the 550 Maranello was a completely new design from its mid-engine predecessors. Unlike the Boxer and Testarossa which had a 180 degree "flat-12" engine, the 550 Maranello has a proper V12 engine with 5.5 litres (hence "550"), producing 485HP.

I expected the car to be torquey and fast, to sound fantastic, and to have great gear shifts – all trademarks of a flagship V12 Ferrari. However, I could not help but also expect it to be a very disconnected car, with comfort over sensation. That is because grand tourers from the late 1990s to the early 2000s, were all like that. They were not furious, but comfortable and effortless, just like the Murciélago we reviewed. Turning the key, the exhaust roar is impressive, but

我從來都不支持前法拉利總裁 Luca di Montezemolo 將法拉利旗艦 12 缸車型恢復到前置引擎佈局的決定。經過 23 年中置引擎 Berlinetta Boxer 和 Testarossa 的完美佈局之後，前置引擎的 550 Maranello 於 1996 年面世。

Luca di Montezemolo 決心改良旗艦車型，使其更加實用和舒適，而這正是前置引擎佈局所能成就的。由於引擎位於前面並與後面的波箱分離，引擎的重心較低，整體前後重量分佈更加平均。更重要的是，由於設有傳統的後置儲物箱，行李和高爾夫球袋等物品都可以妥當地放入其中，適合橫跨大陸的公路旅行（這輛車被設計成豪華巡航跑車）。法拉利從 1996 年到 2001 年僅生產棍波的 550 Maranello，總產量為 3,083 輛，使其成為今時今日一輛罕見的車。

550 Maranello 的引擎是全新設計的，與其中置引擎的「前輩」完全不同。不像 Boxer 和 Testarossa 採用的 180 度「水平對向 12 缸」引擎，550 Maranello 採用了一個 5.5 公升容量的正統 V12 引擎（因此被稱為「550」），輸出 485 匹馬力。

我預期這輛車會有扭力和速度感，會聽起來很棒，轉波會很順暢——這些都是旗艦 V12 法拉利的標誌。然而，我不禁也會預期這輛車會是一輛無感覺的車，舒適凌駕於感受。因為從 20 世紀 90 年代末到 21 世紀初的豪華巡航跑車都是這個樣子。它們並不狂野，卻是舒適而輕鬆的，就像我們評測的 Murciélago 一樣。轉動鑰匙，排氣管的轟鳴聲令人印象深刻，但這僅僅由於這輛汽車裝有 Tubi 排氣系統。在 F430 和 599 GTB 之前的燃油噴注式法拉利通常配備的原廠排氣系統聲音都相對柔和。

啟動車子時，離合器不算輕，但也不會妨礙操作。駕駛這輛車的感覺對我來說非常熟悉，從試車的頭兩米開始就覺得一見如故。新引入的風油軚也

that is only because this particular car has Tubi exhausts. The fuel injected Ferrari's prior to the F430 and 599 GTB generation were generally muted with their original exhausts.

Setting off, the clutch is not light but not obstructive either. It is easy to fetter with and I felt right at home from the first two metres of my test drive. The introduction of power steering is also much welcomed. Stepping on it, the engine sounds wonderful as anticipated, but admittedly it does not sound as raw or as vigorous as its flat-12 predecessors. The car is fast on the straights, but straight line speed is not the forte of the car. Surprisingly, it is when the corners started arriving that the car really starts to shine. Despite being a big grand tourer, the car really found its place in corners. It is very balanced, the brakes are good, and it is extremely steady, allowing you to brake and position yourself just where you want the car to be without any fuss, before throwing it into the corner confidently. The size of the car also miraculously shrinks when you are driving it aggressively from one tight corner to the next. Period journalists accurately described it as an "exploitable super car".

The 550 Maranello is a really special car, and although it will never look as beautiful to me as its mid-engine elders, it will always be recognised as one of Ferrari's all-time greats thanks to its all-rounded charms. The way it was able to transform from a comfortable grand tourer into a capable performance car instantly when a corner arrived, was truly incredible.

很受歡迎。踩油門時，引擎聲音如預期般美妙，但坦白地說，它的聲音並不像其他水平對向12缸車系那麼原始或充滿活力。這輛車的直線速度很快，但這不是它的強項。令人驚訝的是，當開始轉彎時，車輛真的開始發揮其優勢。儘管是一輛大型豪華巡航跑車，但它在彎道中的表現非常出色。車子非常平衡，剎車效果良好，非常穩定，讓你能夠輕鬆地剎車和調整車輛位置，然後自信地轉入彎道。當你從一個急彎駛到下一個急彎時，這輛車的尺寸也神奇地縮小了。那時代的記者準確地描述它為「實用的超級跑車」。

550 Maranello 是一輛非常特別的車，雖然在我眼中它永遠不會像其他中置引擎車系那樣漂亮，但由於它擁有全方位的魅力，將永遠被譽為法拉利史上其中一件最偉大的作品。它能夠在彎道來臨時，瞬間從舒適的豪華巡航跑車轉變為性能出眾的跑車，真令人難以置信。

Production Years: 1971-1975
Engine: Fuel injected 2.9 twin turbocharged V8; 478HP
Total Production: 1,315 units

生產年份：1971-1975
引擎：燃油噴注 2.9 雙渦輪增壓 V8；478 匹馬力
總產量：1,315 輛

Owner's remarks:

The one and only F40. A young man's dream come true. The sound, soul, rawness and the uncompromising nature of the car are breathtaking and everything I have imagined. Timeless shape with unique details in the design, just a stationary F40 is a sight to be savoured.

車主的話：

一輛獨一無二的 F40。它令年輕人的夢想成真。它的聲音、靈魂、純真和不妥協的本質令人驚嘆，完全超出我的想像。永恆的外形，配以獨特的設計細節，即使是靜止的 F40 也令人賞心悅目。

Ferrari 法拉利 F40 (1992)

The Ferrari Big 5 are special models that Ferrari releases every few years to showcase the pinnacle of their cars at the time. While the later Big 5 models like the Enzo and LaFerrari were purely a power flex and a preview to the world of new technology that they can expect to see in their regular production models to come, the early Big 5 cars had more of a racing purpose. In the early 1980s when Ferrari developed the 288 GTO, they had the intention of joining the Group B racing series. The Group B racing series was kind of a Wild West racing series where pretty much anything goes (aside from engine capacity limitations – 4 litre for naturally aspirated cars and 2.8 litre for turbocharged cars).

Ferrari ended up building 272 units of the 288 GTO in order to meet the homologation requirement of 200 units. In addition to that, they built 5 units of the 288 GTO Evoluzione which was the hardcore racing version with huge spoilers, 650HP (over the ordinary 288 GTO's 400HP), and only 950KG. Unfortunately, right after Ferrari finished developing the 288 GTO Evoluzione, the Group B racing series was cancelled and never took off. Enzo Ferrari, finding himself with 5 race cars that became obsolete overnight, decided to have his engineers design a super Ferrari road car based on the 288 GTO Evoluzione. That ultimately gave birth to not only the F40, but also Ferrari's crusade to building the Big 5. Ferrari engineers were only given 12 months to create the F40, as the car was intended to celebrate Ferrari's 40th anniversary at the time in 1987. Thankfully, his engineers made the deadline, as the F40 turned out to be the last Ferrari that Enzo himself approved and also presented to

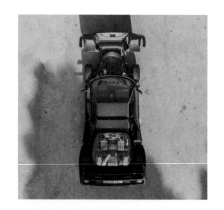

Ferrari Big 5 是法拉利每隔幾年便會推出的特殊車型，以展示其車輛的巔峰水平。而後期的 Big 5 車型，如 Enzo 和 LaFerrari，純粹是炫耀動力和展示未來常規生產車型的新技術。而早期的 Big 5 車型則更多用於賽車場上的目的。在 1980 年代初，當法拉利開發 288 GTO 時，他們有意加入 B 組賽車系列。B 組賽車系列有點像狂野西部賽車系列，幾乎不設任何限制（除了有引擎排量限制——自然進氣車 4 公升，渦輪增壓車 2.8 公升）。

法拉利最終生產了 272 輛 288 GTO，以滿足生產 200 輛公路車型的 B 組賽車系列官方要求。此外，他們還生產了 5 輛 288 GTO Evoluzione 的高性能賽車版本，配有巨大尾翼，650 匹馬力（超過普通 288 GTO 的 400 匹馬力），並且只重 950 公斤。不幸的是，就在法拉利完成 288 GTO Evoluzione 的開發後，B 組賽車系列被取消，從此未再啟動。Enzo Ferrari 發現自己手頭上的 5 輛賽車一夜之間變得過時，於是決定讓工程師設計一輛建基於 288 GTO Evoluzione 的超級法拉利公路車。這不僅催生了 F40，還開啟了法拉利打造 Big 5 車型的征程。法拉利的工程師只有 12 個月時間來創造 F40，他們在 1987 年想用這款車慶祝法拉利成立 40 週年。幸好，工程師們在期限前完成了任務，F40 最終成為 Enzo 最後親手批核並於 1987 年在 Maranello 親自向媒體展示的一輛法拉利。不久，這位傳奇車廠創始人便去世。

法拉利的目標是製造一輛具有極限性能的合法公路賽車，配備 2.9 公升 V8 雙渦輪增壓引擎（起源於 308），輸出 478 匹馬力。使用碳纖維強化聚合材料來大幅降低車身重量至僅為 1,100 公斤。結果，這輛車能在 3.7 秒內由靜止加速至 60 英里（在 1987 年！），並成為第一輛突破時速 200 英里（達時速 201 英里）的法拉利公路車。

the media in person in Maranello in 1987. Shortly afterwards, the legendary carmaker passed away.

Ferrari's intention was to make a maximum performance street legal race car – with a 2.9 litre V8 twin-turbo engine (which originated from the 308) producing 478HP. Carbon-Kevlar composite material was used extensively to keep the car's weight down to a mere 1,100KG. The result was a car that could achieve 0-60MPH in 3.7 seconds (in 1987!), and the first Ferrari road car to break the 200MPH barrier, at 201MPH.

The moment you enter the F40 you immediately know it is an uncompromising car, with a tall side sill that you must carefully navigate over, to avoid scratching the carbon fibre, before dropping yourself into the seat. The foot pedals are off-centred to the right, and a quick look at the footwell reminds me that the reason for this are the relatively wide front wheels that take up a lot of footwell space. The clutch is quite heavy, and the biting point is a lot shorter than other road cars, reminding me once again that this is a street legal race car. In any event, setting off was manageable after slotting the familiar open gated five-speed manual gearbox into its dog leg first gear.

In motion, the suspension is bumpy but reasonable. Like what a proper street legal race car should be, everything is heavy and hard: the gear changes require some muscles, the steering is heavy but also very direct and communicative, and the brakes are decent but squeaks loudly once warmed up. But you will forget all of that when you squeeze the throttle and hear that glorious V8 engine that doesn't sound like any other Ferrari's I have ever driven. Power delivery is not the ECU-managed linear feel that we get in modern turbocharged Ferrari's, but rough, vocal, and confrontational. The only surprise was that, despite the age of the car and the lack of sound deadening, there were not much rattles or road noise that I noticed.

These days, a "street legal race car" is merely a gimmick that is more imagination than reality, given the constraints of stringent road safety regulations. A 430 Scuderia may have a similar bare-looking interior and a 488 GTB may have a similarly twin-turbocharged V8 engine, but they will never hold a candle to the purity and outright insanity of the F40.

當你進入這輛 F40 時，立刻就會知道這是一輛毫不妥協的車，有一個很高的門檻，必須小心翼翼地跨過，以免刮損碳纖維，然後才能坐進車內。瞥見踏板區，稍微偏向右側，我想這是由於相對寬闊的前輪佔用了大量腳部空間。離合器非常沉重，咬合點比其他公路車要短得多，再次提醒我這是一輛合法的公路賽車。將熟悉的 dog leg 格式五速手動波箱進入一波後，起動起來並不困難。

行駛時，避震系統有些顛簸但還算合理。就像一輛真正的合法公路賽車，一切都很沉重和堅硬：轉波需要一些氣力，轉向沉重但非常直接和有力，剎車還不錯但熱身後會發出尖銳的嘎吱聲。但當你踩下油門，聽到那種無比美妙的 V8 引擎聲音時，你將忘記一切，它的聲音與我駕駛過的其他法拉利都不同。動力傳遞並不像現代渦輪增壓的法拉利提供的那種由引擎電腦控制管理的線性感覺，而是粗獷、響亮，而且充滿對抗性。唯一令人驚訝的是，儘管車齡較大且欠缺隔音，但我幾乎沒有注意到嘎吱聲或路面噪音。

如今，因為嚴格的道路安全法規限制，「合法的公路賽車」僅是一個噱頭，只是想像而非現實。430 Scuderia 可能具有類似的簡潔內飾，488 GTB 或許配備相似的雙渦輪增壓 V8 引擎，但它們永遠無法與 F40 的純淨和徹底的瘋狂相比擬。

Production Years (for the 3.8 Series 1 only): 1961-1964	生產年份（僅限於 3.8 Series 1）：1961-1964
Engine: Carburetted 3.8 inline 6; 265HP	引擎：化油器 3.8 直列 6 缸；265 匹馬力
Total Production (for the 3.8 Series 1 Roadster only): 7,828 units	總產量（僅限於 3.8 Series 1 敞篷跑車）：7,828 輛

Owner's remarks:

I always wanted a Jaguar E-Type as it is an absolutely iconic shape. I also knew that it had to be an open top Series 1. I have owned my Jaguar over 12 years and it is still an absolute joy sitting behind the straight six engine which quietly burbles under the gorgeous long bonnet which simply seems to go on forever.

Of course, like any 60-year-old car it has its problem, but it is also relatively easy to maintain and any spare part is easily available on the internet.

車主的話：

我一直想擁有一輛積架 E-Type，因為它是一款絕對具標誌性的車型。我也知道必須是一輛敞篷的 Series 1。我擁有這輛積架已經超過 12 年了，坐在那靈魂充沛的直列 6 缸引擎後面仍然令人感到愉悦。它在華麗的長引擎蓋下低語着，看似永無止境。

當然，像任何 60 年的老爺車一樣，它也有自身的問題，但維修相對容易，任何配件都可以在網上輕易找到。

Jaguar 積架
E-Type 3.8 Series 1 Roadster
E-Type 3.8 Series 1 敞篷版
(1963)

Enzo Ferrari allegedly described the Jaguar E-Type as the most beautiful car ever made when it was launched in 1961. While I am not sure how true that rumour is, I think it does not really matter whether he said it or not, as most people will agree that the Jaguar E-Type is one of the most beautiful cars ever made.

The Jaguar E-Type was based on the hugely successful Jaguar D-Type racer, which won the 24 Hours Le Man for three consecutive years between 1955 to 1957. Having such big shoes to fill, the E-Type is no snail. It has a 3.8 straight six carburetted engine producing 265HP – a very impressive figure at the time (and not exactly embarrassing now). Its top speed is 150MPH (240KMH), which was apparently verified by motor magazines at the time. It was produced between 1961-1975 with three variants – convertible, two-seater hard top (a.k.a. "fixed head"), and four-seater hard top.

The car being reviewed is a 1963 Jaguar E-Type 3.8 Series 1 Roadster. It was originally a left-hand drive US car, which was then brought back to the UK and converted to right-hand drive. That was when the current owner bought it and brought it back to Hong Kong. It is no garage queen – being a frequent contestant in the Classic Car Club of Hong Kong's China rallies.

First time driving this car, I immediately noticed how spacious it was for me. The car looked relatively small from the outside, so the spacious interior was a surprise. Visibility, like most classic cars with thin a-pillars and huge windscreens, is very good; except the internal rearview mirror could be bigger. The pedal positions are good, and the clutch is light and easy to control.

在 1961 年積架 E-Type 發佈時，據說 Enzo Ferrari 曾將其形容為有史以來最漂亮的車。雖然我不確定這個傳聞是否屬實，但我認為他有沒有這樣說過並不重要，因為大多數人都會同意積架 E-Type 是有史以來最漂亮的車之一。

積架 E-Type 建基於非常成功的積架 D-Type 賽車，該賽車在 1955 年至 1957 年連續三年贏得了利曼 24 小時耐力賽。面對如此高的期望，E-Type 絕對不是一輛緩慢的車。它擁有 3.8 公升直列 6 缸化油器引擎，輸出 265 匹馬力——這在當時是令人印象非常深刻的數字（現在看來也毫不遜色）。它的最高時速為每小時 150 英里（每小時 240 公里），當時的汽車雜誌也驗證了這一數據。它在 1961 年至 1975 年間生產了三個版本——敞篷車、兩座硬頂車（也稱為「固定頭」）和四座硬頂車。

這裏評測的是一輛 1963 年的積架 E-Type 3.8 Series 1 敞篷跑車。它最初是一輛左軚美國車，後來被運回英國並改為右軚。當時的車主購買後把它帶回香港。但它不是躺在車房裏的收藏品——它經常參加香港老爺車會的中國拉力賽。

第一次駕駛這輛車時，我立刻注意到它有多寬敞。從外面看，這輛車看起來相對小巧，所以寬敞的內部讓我感到驚喜。像大多數配備細 A 柱和巨大擋風玻璃的老爺車，它的視野非常寬闊；只是內部後視鏡可以更大一些。踏板的位置很好，離合器輕巧且易於控制。

要啟動這輛車，可按一下儀表盤正中央的起動按鈕，這是頗劃時代的特點。E-Type 的動力輸出並不像現代車那樣具爆發性，而是平穩而充足。踩下油門時，你真的能感受到車子的輕盈。然而，在我短暫的駕駛中，有一件很難適應的事情——波箱。不是由於一波缺乏同步器，因為這代表你不能在車子完全停下前從二波轉回一波（無論如何，在駕駛老爺車時你應該避免這樣做），而是因為波與波之

To start the car, there is a starter button right at the middle of the dashboard, a feature that was ahead of its time. The power delivery of the E-Type is not explosive as with modern cars, but is certainly smooth and ample. You really do feel the lightness of the car when stepping on it. One thing that was hard to get used to in my short drive, however, was the gearbox. Not so much the lack of synchromesh in the first gear, as that simply means you cannot go from second gear to first before the car is fully stopped (something you should generally avoid in classic cars anyway), but more the way the gears are placed. The Series 1 E-Type has a four-speed gearbox in the conventional H pattern. The issue is that the throws are very long, and the gears are very close together. I was warned by the owner before I set off that it is easy to get into reverse when trying to go into first. And guess which direction I went right after that? Not forward. With that experience, it immediately made me nervous when going from first to second (as I may go from first to fourth), or worse yet, accidentally going from second to first at high rev! However, I believe these are things that you can easily get used to if you own the car.

Overall, the driving experience of the E-Type was very memorable, even though the car is not the easiest to get used to immediately. If I must have one complaint, it would be that the engine and exhaust note of the straight six engine is a little underwhelming. Other than that, this car is true automotive perfection, which is something that only happens once every few decades, hence its undisputed legendary status.

間的位置。Series 1 E-Type 配備傳統的四速波箱 H 型配置。問題在於轉波的行程非常長,波與波之間的位置卻非常接近。在啟動車子前車主警告我,轉到一波時很容易進入後波。猜猜之後我是往哪個方向走的?不是向前。由於有這種經歷,我從一波轉到二波時立刻緊張起來(我可能會從一波轉到四波),或者更糟的是,意外地在高轉速時從二波轉回一波!不過,相信如果你擁有這輛車,這些都是可以輕鬆適應的事情。

總括而言,E-Type 的駕駛體驗令人非常難忘,儘管這輛車不是最容易令人適應的車。如果我必須抱怨,那就是直列 6 缸引擎和排氣聲音略顯乏味。除此之外,這輛車可說是完美之作,更是幾十年一遇的。這造就了其毋容置疑的傳奇地位。

Production Year: 2003
Engine: Fuel injected 6.2 V12; 580HP
Total Production: 50 units

生產年份： 2003
引擎：燃油噴注 6.2 V12；580 匹馬力
總產量：50 輛

Owner's remarks:

Upon stepping into the Murciélago, the distinct feeling of beasty heaviness is unmistakable and thus the reason for the exhilaration and assurance every time I start driving it. Its 2003 birth year does not hinder its ability to compete with its more modern rivals in terms of its mechanical and engaging responsiveness. Today, the car continues to surprise me and gives me an unwavering elation, even after owning it for almost 20 years. I am never able to find the same enjoyment from driving any other vehicle.

車主的話：

一踏進 Murciélago，那種野獸般的沉重感是無可避免的，這也是我每次開車時會產生興奮和肯定的原因。即使它在 2003 年誕生，但它在機械性能和駕駛反應方面，並不比更現代的競爭對手遜色。至今，這輛車仍然給我帶來驚喜，讓我在擁有它將近 20 年後依然有着的愉悅感。我再也無法從駕駛其他車輛中找到相同的樂趣。

Lamborghini 林寶基尼
Murciélago 40th Anniversary
Murciélago 40 週年紀念版
(2003)

Unlike Ferrari, Lamborghini never retired their mid-engine V12 flagship line, which they invented back in the late 1960s with the Miura. The Murciélago being the third iteration since the Miura, was produced when Lamborghini was under Audi's ownership, but you would be wrong to think it is a "German Lamborghini" that has lost most of its Italian heritage. The Murciélago does not depart far from its immediate predecessor, the Diablo 6.0. Most importantly, the 6.2L V12 that it uses has practically the same DNA as the original 12-cylinder engine found in the company's first ever model – the 350 GT. The original engine was designed by Italian auto industry heavyweight, Giotto Bizzarrini.

The car being reviewed here is extra special, as it is the 40th anniversary edition. As the name suggests, it was built to celebrate the brand's 40th anniversary. As a special edition, it has a number of things that were made especially for it, such as the colour – a greenish blue known as Verde Artemis created only for the 40th anniversary model. Performance-wise, the 40th anniversary did not gain much upgrades from the already very capable ordinary model; it does have a special exhaust system though. Lamborghini only made 50 units of the 40th anniversary worldwide, all in manual transmission, and the one we are reviewing here is the only one in Hong Kong.

Setting off, you immediately notice two things. First is that the clutch is extremely light. It is also very easy to engage, without any need for getting used to. Despite the Ferrari-like metal and open gated gear shifter, the gear shifts feel soft and liquid. To be honest, the car, looking like the way it does, can

與法拉利不同，林寶堅尼從未停止生產中置引擎 V12 旗艦車型，這一系列最早可以追溯到上世紀 60 年代的 Miura。Murciélago 是自 Miura 以來的第三代車型，是在林寶堅尼於奧迪旗下時生產的，但你如果認為它是一輛失去大部份意大利傳統的「德國林寶堅尼」，那就錯了。Murciélago 與其直系前輩 Diablo 6.0 差別不大。最重要的是，它使用的 6.2 公升 V12 引擎與該公司首款車型 350 GT 的原始 12 缸引擎帶有相同的基因，這款原始引擎是由意大利汽車業界權威 Giotto Bizzarrini 設計的。

這裏評測的這輛車異常特別，因為它是 40 週年紀念版。顧名思義，它是為了慶祝品牌成立 40 週年而誕生的。作為特別版，有一些專為它而設的東西，例如獨特的顏色——一種僅為 40 週年紀念版出產的藍綠色，被稱為 Verde Artemis。在性能方面，40 週年紀念版與已經非常出色的普通車型相比，並沒有太多升級，但它擁有一個特別為它而設的排氣系統。林寶堅尼在全球只生產了 50 輛 40 週年紀念版，全為棍波版，而這裏評測的這輛是香港唯一的一輛。

啟動車子時，你立刻會注意到兩件事。首先是離合器非常輕。它也很容易啟動，不需要適應。儘管有像法拉利一樣的金屬和外露式檔閘波棍設計，但轉波感覺柔軟順暢。老實說，這輛車看起來，稍微重一點的離合器和更堅實的轉波會較配合它的外觀。其次，不那麼令人驚訝的是車身寬度。在你啟動車子的那一刻，你需要經常查看左右後視鏡，以確保你在車道內。

但是，一旦你踩下油門，其他一切都不重要了。那種令人讚嘆的 V12 聲音正是我所預期的。意大利 V12 引擎的咆哮聲無與倫比，儘管在車廂內聽起來有些沉默，這可能需要改裝排氣系統以作改善。一如預期，憑藉 580 匹馬力，這輛車非常快，但是它的加速方式更令人難忘。動力和速度上升得非常迅

benefit from a slightly heavier clutch and more rigid gear shifts to go with its look. The second thing, and something which is less of a surprise here, is the car's width. Literally the moment you set off you keep looking at your left and right mirrors to make sure you are within your lane.

The moment you step on the gas pedal though, nothing else matters. That glorious V12 sound is everything I had anticipated it to be. The Italian V12 roar can be rivalled by nothing else, although admittedly it does sound a little muted in the cabin and can benefit from an aftermarket exhaust. As expected, with 580HP, the car is fast, but it is the way it picks up that is impressive. Power and speed pick up very quickly, as if you were driving a very light car, which is hardly the case as the car is 1,800KG+. This must have certainly been due to the car's four-wheel drive system, making the power surge rapid and effortless.

The fact that at speed, the car feels very much like a grand tourer (because it is one), was an odd feeling. Because while visually, the car looks like a racing-esque sports car on steroids, the sensation it provides at speed is a lot more muted and mature, as a grand tourer should be. Although that should have been expected, it nevertheless felt awkward and out of character when I got off the car and looked back at its amazing physical presence.

速,就像你在駕駛一輛非常輕的車,然而實際上這輛車的重量超過 1,800 公斤。這肯定是有賴四輪驅動系統,使動力增加迅速且毫不費力。

事實上,在高速行駛時,這輛車感覺上與一輛豪華巡航跑車(它本來就是)非常相似,這種感覺很奇怪。因為這輛車雖然看起來像一輛超級跑車,但在高速行駛時感覺卻更加柔和與成熟,就像一輛真正豪華巡航跑車。雖然這點不出所料,但當我下車回頭看着這輛車令人驚嘆的外觀時,仍然感到奇怪和始料未及。

Production Years (for the Series 2 only): 1966-1969   生產年份（僅限於 Series 2）：1966-1969
Engine: Carburetted 4.7 V8; 286HP   引擎：化油器 4.7 V8；286 匹馬力
Total Production (for the Series 2 only): 500 units   總產量（僅限於 Series 2）：500 輛

Owner's remarks:

The first time I met and touched the Maserati Quattroporte 1 in person was when I was invited by Modena to a gathering celebrating the Maserati Centennial back in September 2014. The Quattroporte is undoubtedly the authentic ancestor of today's sports sedans, and definitely a milestone of the automobile industry. Owning this Quattroporte is a true pride and dream since it is now an honour in my hand to safeguard this remarkable piece of automobile history. Not long ago, my Maestro, Adolfo Orsi Jr., the son of Omar Orsi who was the second owner of the Maserati empire after the Maserati family, and the original proposer and designer of the Quattroporte, excavated from the Maserati Classiche archive some of his father's valuable handwritten papers with details on preparing my Quattroporte for the London Earl's Court Motor Show in 1969. This precious find is a little treasure for both Maestro Adolfo and his "scolaro" Edwin!

The Quattroporte 1 engine, the derivative of the famous 450S V8 engine, is a true racing blood. It naturally gives whoever behind the wheel a good sporty driving experience. The car still runs powerfully and fast by today's driving standard, although it is an automatic. If it were not that gas consuming, and for the worry of overheating under Hong Kong's weather, it could be a great daily driving car!

車主的話：

我第一次親身接觸瑪莎拉蒂 Quattroporte 1 是在 2014 年 9 月，那時我被邀請參加慶祝瑪莎拉蒂在意大利摩德納百週年紀念的聚會。Quattroporte 無疑是現今運動轎車的真正始祖，也絕對是汽車工業的里程碑。擁有這輛 Quattroporte 是一種真正的自豪也是一個夢想，因為我很榮幸能夠守護這一非凡的汽車歷史。不久前，我的導師 Adolfo Orsi Jr.（他是瑪莎拉蒂家族後繼者 Omar Orsi 的兒子，也是 Quattroporte 的原始提議者和設計師）從瑪莎拉蒂 Classiche 檔案中找出他父親的珍貴手稿，其中詳細介紹了為我這部 Quattroporte 於 1969 年倫敦伯爵府車展做準備的細節。這一珍貴的發現對導師 Adolfo Orsi Jr. 和他的「學徒」 Edwin 來説都是一個小寶藏！

Quattroporte 1 的引擎是著名的 450S V8 引擎的衍生品，是真正的賽車血統。無論誰駕駛這輛車，都會得到良好的運動駕駛體驗。即使是一輛自動波車，但在現今的駕駛標準下仍然運作強勁和迅猛。如果它不是那麼耗油，又不用擔心香港氣溫過高，它可是一輛非常適合日常駕駛的車！

Maserati 瑪莎拉蒂
Quattroporte 1 (Series 2)
(1969)

"Quattroporte" in Italian literally means four doors which was why Maserati used this name for their first ever four-door saloon car. Already known for making great GT cruiser cars at the time, Maserati decided it was only right to produce a four-door model for their customers to travel across the continent with family and friends more comfortably.

The first generation of the Quattroporte is commonly referred to as the Quattroporte 1. Maserati made two versions of it; the Series 1 from 1963 to 1966 and the Series 2 from 1966 to 1969. The car we have here is a Series 2. Maserati made a total of 776 Quattroporte 1's, 500 of which were the Series 2. The car we are reviewing is a right-hand drive version, making it even rarer. This is also the only Quattroporte 1 registered in Hong Kong, if not the only one that resides here. Furthermore, this particular Quattroporte 1 was the actual show car that Maserati displayed at the London Motor Show in Earl's Court back in 1969, which explains why it has eye-catching options like a two-tone body colour and rearview mirrors on both sides (rare option for that era).

Sitting inside the car, I found the comfortable leather and prestigious wooden trim were as expected. However, there were a few interesting things that I did not expect. The dash layout is very similar to that of the Jaguar E-Type, with all the buttons and switches gathered in the middle. The side indicator (and air horn) stalk is on the right side like a Japanese car. And finally, the gear stick that operates the Borg Warner 3-speed automatic transmission goes from Park to Drive from the bottom up, and not the other way around as with conventional cars.

意大利文「Quattroporte」意味着四道門，這就是瑪莎拉蒂為他們的第一輛四門轎車冠以這個名字的原因。當時瑪莎拉蒂已因生產出色的巡航跑車而聞名，他們之後決定生產一款四門車型，讓顧客能更舒適地與家人和朋友穿州過省旅行。

第一代 Quattroporte 通常被稱為 Quattroporte 1。瑪莎拉蒂總共生產了兩個版本：1963 年至 1966 年的 Series 1 和 1966 年至 1969 年的 Series 2。這次評測的車型是 Series 2。瑪莎拉蒂一共生產了 776 輛 Quattroporte 1，其中 500 輛是 Series 2。這輛車是右軚版本，極其罕有。這也是唯一一輛在香港註冊的 Quattroporte 1，也很大可能是唯一一輛駐留在香港的 Quattroporte 1。此外，這輛 Quattroporte 1 是瑪莎拉蒂在 1969 年倫敦伯爵府車展上展示的實際展品，這解釋了為何它具有引人注目的雙色車身和兩側後視鏡（這在當時是罕見的）。

坐在車裏，一如所料，我看到了舒適的皮革和莊重的木質飾板。但有幾件我沒有預料到的有趣事物。儀表盤佈局與積架 E-Type 非常相似，所有的按鈕和開關都集中在中央。指揮燈（和響號）的操縱桿位於右側，就像日本車。最後，用於操作 Borg Warner 三速自動波箱的波桿從下而上由 P 波切換至 D 波，不像常規車輛那樣由上而下。

Series 2 Quattroporte 1 採用瑪莎拉蒂標誌性的 Tipo 107 4.7 公升 V8 引擎，具有雙頂置凸輪軸和四個雙喉噴嘴 Weber 化油器（早期版本採用了 4.1 公升引擎）。該引擎可產生 286 匹馬力，使 Quattroporte 成為當時世界上最快的轎車。作為一款用於長途旅行的豪華轎車，我曾擔心瑪莎拉蒂會為了舒適度而壓抑引擎和排氣聲音。幸好情況並非如此。該輛車聽起來像我的 Indy 一樣肯定和強大。乘坐體驗也很好，瑪莎拉蒂沒有過份致力使其成為舒適的轎車，故沒配置吸震筒懸掛系統等設施。Series 2

The Series 2 Quattroporte 1 uses Maserati's iconic Tipo 107 4.7 V8 engine with double overhead camshafts and four twin-choke Weber carburettors (earlier versions used a 4.1 engine). The engine generates 286HP, making the Quattroporte the fastest saloon car in the world at the time. Being a luxury saloon car intended for long distance travels, I had feared that Maserati would muffle the engine and exhaust note of that magnificent engine in exchange for comfort. Fortunately, that was not the case. The car sounds as assertive and as potent as my Indy. Same goes for the ride, Maserati did not make much effort to make it a comfortable saloon with hydraulic suspensions or anything like that. The Series 2 Quattroporte 1 does not have rear independent suspension, Maserati opted for solid axle with leaf springs instead. The ride was therefore firmer than expected, but not uncomfortable.

From the outside, the Quattroporte looks like a gentleman in an expensive designer suit, but the moment you step on the gas pedal the inner beast of the car comes alive with that unmistakable Tipo 107 V8 roar followed by violent pops and bangs from the twin exhaust pipes – just brilliant!

Quattroporte 1 也沒有配備獨立的後避震,而是選擇了實心軸和片狀彈簧。因此,乘坐感覺比預期堅實,但不會不舒適。

從外觀上,Quattroporte 看起來像一位穿着高級西裝的紳士,但當你踩下油門踏板時,車內的野獸就會甦醒,伴隨着明顯的 Tipo 107 V8 轟鳴聲,隨後是雙排氣管的猛烈爆裂聲——真是太棒了!

Production Years (for the 4.7 version only): 1970-1973
Engine: Carburetted 4.7 V8; 290HP
Total Production (for the 4.7 version only): 364 units

生產年份（僅限於 4.7 版本）：1970-1973
引擎：化油器 4.7 V8；290 匹馬力
總產量（僅限於 4.7 版本）：364 輛

Owner's remarks:

There is something about the sound, smell, and feel of a 1960s or 1970s Italian classic car that cannot be rivalled by cars of any other eras. I have always wanted to own a big-engined Italian classic and this Maserati fulfilled my dream – it is exactly everything I have hoped for. Its wedge-shaped design, by Vignale, gives it a beautiful presence that is rarely achieved by a 2+2 car. Thanks to the previous owner for putting it through a very thorough restoration, the car has been relatively trouble free to live with too.

車主的話：

那些 1960 年代或 1970 年代意大利老爺車的聲音、氣味和感覺，是其他年代汽車無法比擬的。我一直想擁有一輛馬力大的意大利老爺車，而這輛瑪莎拉蒂完全滿足了我的願望——它正是我所期望的一切。由 Vignale 經手的楔形設計賦予其華麗的外觀，這是 2+2 汽車很少能達到的。感謝前任車主對它進行了非常徹底的修復，這輛車在日常駕駛時幾乎沒有甚麼問題。

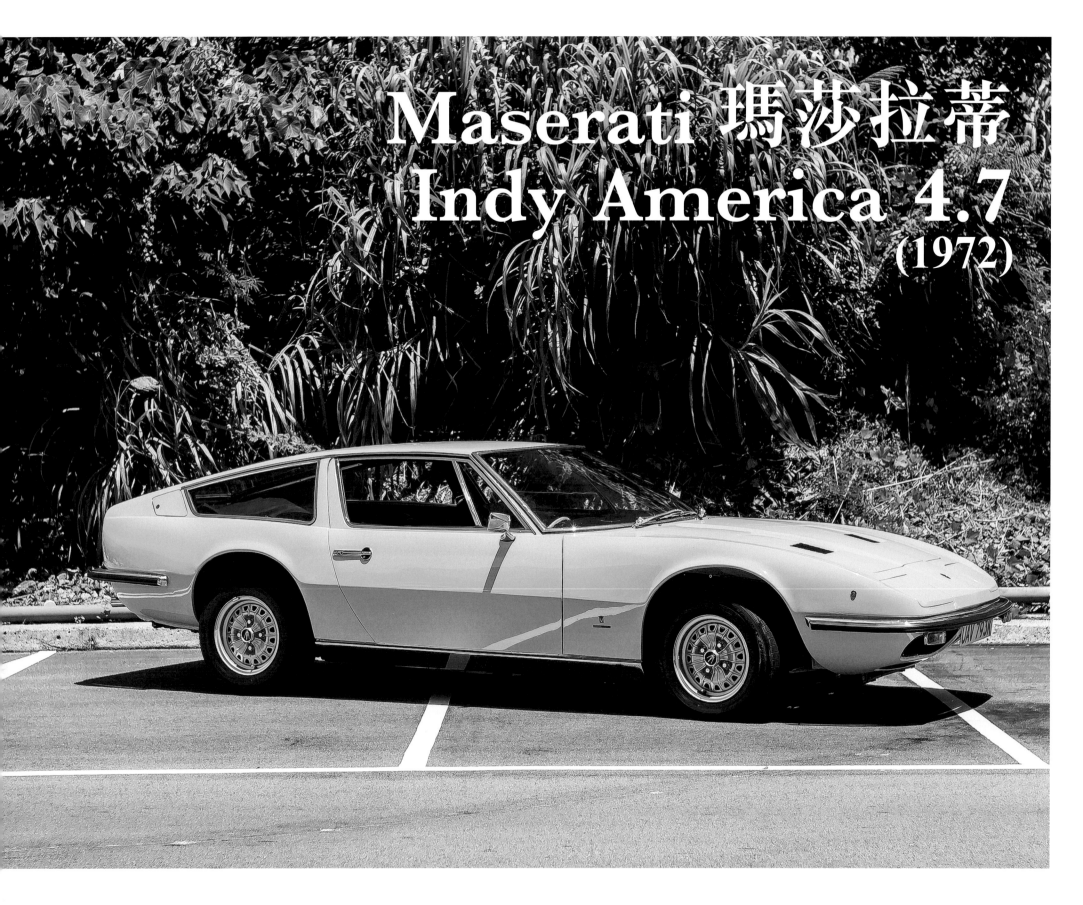

Maserati 瑪莎拉蒂 Indy America 4.7
(1972)

I still remember the first time I saw this car. It was at the 2016 Classic Car Club of Hong Kong's annual lunch at the Hong Kong Jockey Club Beas River clubhouse. It caught my attention immediately and I ran across the lawn to take a better look at this mysterious but obviously Italian car. I quickly learnt that it was a Maserati Indy America, imported from the UK by a local second-hand dealer. Shortly after that fateful day, my good friend, Keith Martin, bought this very car at an auction, after perhaps one too many beers. The car turned out to be in pretty bad condition; not in its original colour, lots of rust, and a badly trimmed interior. This began Keith's long and costly restoration process, which brought the car from Hong Kong to the UK, and back to Hong Kong again.

The good news is that after a two-year, multi-country restoration, the car is now in top condition and is probably one of the most sorted Indy America's in the world. It is also the Indy America that I got to review.

The official headline regarding the Indy's birth was to celebrate Maserati's successful racer, the 8CTF, which won the Indy 500 twice in a row, in 1939 and 1940 (hence the Indy's name). The actual reason was that it was produced as a four-seater to provide buyers an alternative to the beautiful first generation Maserati Ghibli (AM115), which was a two-seater produced around the same period between 1967-1973.

Maserati made about 1,100 Indy's. All of them were V8's with four overhead camshaft and four twin-choke down-draught Weber carburettors. Throughout production, engine capacity slowly increased from 4.2 to 4.7, and to its final iteration of 4.9. The subject car

我還記得第一次看到這輛車的情景。那是在 2016 年，當時我參加了香港老爺車會在香港賽馬會雙魚河鄉村會所舉辦的週年午宴。這輛神秘但明顯是意大利生產的車立刻吸引了我的注意，我跑過草坪去細看，很快得知它是一輛瑪莎拉蒂 Indy America，由當地的二手車經銷商從英國進口。在那個命中注定的日子後不久，我的好朋友 Keith Martin 在一次拍賣會中買下了這輛車，當時他可能喝了太多啤酒。這輛車的狀況非常糟糕：車身不是原廠的顏色、有很多鏽漬、內部狀態也非常不濟。Keith 由此展開了長期且昂貴的修復過程。他將這輛車從香港運往英國修復，然後再運回香港再修復。

幸好，輾轉經過兩年多的多國修復，這輛車現在已處於最佳狀態，並可能是全球最完美的 Indy America 汽車之一。這也是我將評測的車。

關於 Indy 誕生的官方新聞，是為了慶祝瑪莎拉蒂成功的賽車 8CTF，該車在 1939 年和 1940 年連續兩次贏得了印第安納波利斯 500 英里大獎賽冠軍（因此得名 Indy）。但實際原因是，它是漂亮的第一代瑪莎拉蒂 Ghibli（AM115）四座位版本，Ghibli 是 1967 年至 1973 年間生產的兩座位跑車。

瑪莎拉蒂生產了約 1,100 輛 Indy。全部配備了四個頂置凸輪軸和四個雙喉噴嘴下吸式 Weber 化油器 V8 引擎。在生產過程中，引擎容量逐漸增加，從 4.2 公升增加到 4.7 公升，最後達到 4.9 公升。這輛車是 4.7 公升版本。

坐在車裏，你會發現四面八方的視野都很開闊，像這個時代的大多數車輛，A 柱很窄。手掣位於左側下方，幾乎就在方向盤下方，位於中控台和司機座椅之間。離合器出奇地舒適而不沉重，波棍短而穩固，在整個駕駛過程中，進入任何波段都非常暢順。我很高興發現調節離合器非常容易，咬合點和離合器的行程都非常容易控制，不需要進行任何試錯。

is a 4.7 version.

Sitting in the car, you will find visibility from all sides is great, with thin A-pillars like most cars from this era. The handbrake is dipped low on your left side, almost right under the steering wheel and between the centre console and the driver's seat. The clutch is surprisingly civilised and not heavy, and the shifter short and solid, with no drama slotting it into any gears throughout my entire drive. I was pleasantly surprised by how easy it was to modulate the clutch, where the biting point and clutch travel were all very easy to handle with no need for any trial and error.

As we got onto the open roads I was able to open up the car a bit and that carburetted V8 sang beautifully. The sound this car makes is therapeutic. The V8 sounds strong and thunderous, exactly what you would expect from a carburetted Italian V8. However, I was surprised to also notice a hint of American muscle grumble when stepping on it.

The car has good power and torque, but you do feel the size and weight dragging it back. Some cars feel smaller than they look when you are driving them, but not this one. This is not really an issue though, as the ambience of the cockpit, and more importantly, the exhaust note, trump everything else.

Author's note: The above drive review was from the very first time I drove the car, about three years ago when Keith agreed to let me review it. Since then, I have been fortunate enough to acquire the car and after a little over a year's ownership, I am happy to report that I am still as impressed with the car now as I was from my first drive. It really is a delightful and intoxicating car.

在空曠的道路上行駛時，我能夠開始加速，化油器 V8 引擎亦開始發出美妙的聲音。這輛車發出的聲音具療癒性。V8 聽起來強大而雷轟，完全符合大家對意大利化油器 V8 的期望。然而，當我踩油門時，驚訝地發現它還帶有一絲「美式肌肉車」的低沉聲音。

雖然這輛車擁有良好的動力和扭力，但你確實感覺它被尺寸和重量拖累。有些車在你駕駛時會讓你感覺它比外觀小，但這輛車不然。不過，這不是問題，因為車廂的環境，尤其是排氣聲音，比其他一切都重要。

作者備註：上述評測是我大約三年前第一次駕駛這輛車的時候寫的，當時 Keith 同意讓我評測。從那時起，我幸運地收購了這輛車，在擁有它一年多後，我很高興現在對這輛車的印象仍然如第一次駕駛時一樣。這真是一輛令人愉悅和陶醉的車。

Production Year: 1989/2020
Engine: Fuel injected 3.8 flat-6; 375HP
Total Production: N/A

生產年份： 1989/2020
引擎：燃油噴注 3.8 水平對向 6 缸；375 匹馬力
總產量：不適用

Owner's remarks:

I have been lucky enough to own and enjoy various Porsche 911 sport cars over the years. Using them as everyday transport, in historic rallies, plus road events to Beijing and Shanghai they have always performed at the highest levels of reliability and driving pleasure.

The adventure of rebuilding my 1989 911 964 into a Theon Recreation was an extremely satisfying one from various angles. Helping to design the look of the engine bay, the practical and overall blend of the retro torpedo Speedster style mirrors to the rear seats reminiscent of the Porsche 928, it was all highly stimulating for me.

Driving the car with its carbon fibre induced lighter weight and increased horsepower is the cream on the cake, however. Manual boxes are always fun and together with the fantastic feedback through the suspension and steering brings many a grin – then the glorious sounds of the flat-six breathing through advanced velocity stacks and barking out through the sports exhausts – satisfaction is guaranteed.

It is still a classic Porsche 911 but all aspects are distilled, enhanced and improved. Got to love the 911.

車主的話：

多年來，我幸運地擁有並駕駛過多種保時捷 911 型號。不論是作為日常交通工具、參加歷史性拉力賽，或前往北京和上海的公路賽事，它們始終在可靠性和駕駛樂趣上表現出色。

將我的 1989 年 911 964 改造成 Theon 創新版車款，在各方面都是令人十分愜意的過程。協助廠方設計引擎艙的外觀、那復古魚雷「Speedster」風格後視鏡的實用性及整體混合性，及讓人聯想到保時捷 928 的後座，這對我來說都是極大的刺激。

然而，駕駛這輛利用碳纖維減輕重量並提升馬力的汽車是錦上添花。手動波箱總帶來樂趣，再加上避震和轉向系統提供的極佳反饋，讓人不禁咧嘴而笑──接著是水平對向 6 缸引擎通過先進的進氣道驅動和升級排氣系統呼嘯而出的壯麗聲音──那是滿足感的保證。

它仍然是一輛老爺的保時捷 911，但各方面都經過精煉、提升和改進。你定會愛上 911。

Theon Design Porsche
保時捷 911
"HK001"
(1989)

Theon Design is a "restomod" company that focuses exclusively on the Porsche 964 model. It was founded by Englishman Adam Hawley who comes from a rather impressive technical background. He was a designer for 15+ years prior to founding Theon Design, and had stints in the auto industry (including Lotus, BMW, and Jaguar) as well as the aero industry (including working on the Airbus A380).

The original 964 comes with a 3.6 litre naturally aspirated flat-six engine producing around 250HP. Theon Design offers a few different engine upgrades, including a 3.8 litre, a 4.0 litre, and in the near future, a supercharged version. The car we are reviewing here, designated as "HK001", has the 3.8 litre engine producing about 375HP. Aside from the engine capacity increase, Theon Design installed individual throttle bodies, larger fuel injectors, bigger valves, and a brand new exhaust system.

All Theon Design 911's come with fully adjustable KW suspensions. HK001 in particular also has the hydraulic front lift system which is helpful for compact cities like Hong Kong. No carbon brakes are needed for such a light car, so instead larger 964 Turbo brakes are used. The original 964 Carrera weighs about 1,400KG dry while the Theon Design 911 weighs about 1,100KG, shedding off around 250KG. To achieve this, aside from the extensive use of carbon fibre for the body panels, engine bay and interior, Theon Design has also gotten rid of a lot of unnecessary parts. For example, HK001 originally started life as a Carrera 4, but the car is now rear-wheel drive only. What is impressive is that the weight ratio is now 43:57, much improved from the original car.

Theon Design 是一家專注用保時捷 964 型號來「restomod」（復修改裝）的公司。它由擁有令人印象深刻的技術背景的英國人 Adam Hawley 創辦。他在創辦 Theon Design 之前擔任設計師超過 15 年，曾在汽車行業（包括蓮花、寶馬和積架）以及航空工業（包括參與空中巴士 A380 的設計）工作。

原始的 964 配備了一台 3.6 公升自然吸氣水平對向 6 缸引擎，輸出約 250 匹馬力。Theon Design 提供了幾種不同的引擎升級，包括 3.8 公升、4.0 公升版本，並計劃推出增壓版本。我們評測的這輛名為「HK001」的車，安裝了 3.8 公升引擎，輸出約 375 匹馬力。除了增加引擎容量外，Theon Design 還安裝了單獨的油門體、較大的燃油噴注器、更大的氣門，以及全新的排氣系統。

所有 Theon Design 的 911 都配備了可全調式的 KW 避震。HK001 尤其配備了液壓前升降系統，對於香港這種狹小的城市很有用。這輛輕量車不需要碳陶瓷碟剎車，而是使用了更大的 964 Turbo 剎車。原始的 964 Carrera 重量約為 1,400 公斤，而 Theon Design 的 911 重量約為 1,100 公斤，減重約 250 公斤。為了達到這個結果，除了在車身、引擎艙和內飾中廣泛使用碳纖維外，Theon Design 還去掉很多不必要的零件。例如，HK001 最初是一輛 Carrera 4，但現在只是後輪驅動。令人印象深刻的是，現在的重量比例為 43：57，比原車改善不少。Theon Design 通過移動某些零件來實現這一目標，例如將重型空調和風油軚泵從後面移到前面。

啟動車子時，我首先注意到踏板很重。離合器相當沉重，而更令人意外的是，油門也相當扎實。雖然我不介意較重的離合器（事實上，它增加了車輛的特性，提醒你身處一輛老爺車），但可以想像在香港堵車時會面對相當大的挑戰。當車子在怠速或低速時，聽起來不會太大聲，但一旦我踩下油門，

Theon Design achieved this by moving certain parts around, such as relocating the heavy AC and power steering pumps from the rear to the front.

Setting off, the first thing I noticed was how heavy the pedals are. The clutch is quite heavy and rather unexpectedly, the throttle is quite firm. While I do not mind heavier clutches (in fact it gives it more character and reminds you that you are in a classic car), I can imagine it will be quite a task if stuck in Hong Kong traffic. The car actually does not sound too loud from the outside when idling or at low speeds, but once I step on the throttle it transforms into something else. The engine roars into life very loudly, which I welcome wholeheartedly as not many things sound better than a tuned air-cooled flat-six Porsche engine.

When blasting the car through the twisties, it is very easy to position your car nicely before and while attacking a tight corner. The ride is firm, but not to an extent of being irritating, allowing the car to take corners firmly and decisively. The pedals, although heavy, are positioned perfectly for heel and toeing. The gear shifts are great and generally do not draw attention to themselves.

One thing I must note is that, while the car has plenty of power, the way the power is delivered throughout the rev range is not how I have expected. At low revs power does not come strongly, if not a little sluggish, but once the needle passes 3,500RPM it just flies. It is as if the car is turbocharged. There are many instances I have had to consciously look at the rev counter to make sure I will not bounce off the limiter.

This is no doubt a very well thought-out car that is a thrill to drive. The exhaust note alone makes the experience very special and memorable.

聲音就完全改變了。引擎非常響亮地嗚嗚着,我十分喜歡,因為世上沒有太多其他比調校過的風冷水平對向 6 缸保時捷引擎更好聽的聲音。

在山路飛馳時,入彎前及在彎內都非常容易將車子放在合適位置。避震系統很堅實,但不會讓人感到不耐煩,車輛能夠堅定而果斷地進入彎道。雖然踏板很重,但對於轉波來說位置剛好。波棍操作極佳,不會引起不必要的注意。

必須留意,雖然這輛車擁有足夠的動力,但動力在整個轉速範圍內的傳遞方式卻超出我的預期。在低轉速下,動力並不強勁,甚至有點遲緩,但一旦指針超過每分鐘 3,500 轉,它就飛起來了,就如配備了渦輪增壓器。在許多情況下,我必須有意識地看着轉速計,以免觸及轉速限制器。

毫無疑問,這是一輛經過精心設計而且令人興奮的車。僅僅排氣聲就令駕駛經驗變得非常特別和難忘。

Production Year: 1990/2018
Engine: Fuel injected 4.0 flat-6; 390HP
Total Production: N/A

生產年份： 1990/2018
引擎：燃油噴注 4.0 水平對向 6 缸；390 匹馬力
總產量：不適用

Owner's remarks:

There is really little more one can say about Singer's famous "restomod" 964 than what has already been widely reviewed in the motor press. Perhaps one perspective from an owner's point of view is the transformation because I have driven the original donor 964 Targa.

Whilst one never accused Porsche of "shoddy" engineering, the Singer transformation is unrecognisable.

The first impression is the steering: so much sharper and tighter. The gearbox has this sprung bolt-like precision motion. Body control and braking performance are on another level…and that engine: now 4.0 litre with a spine-tingling air-cooled soundtrack. Every drive is a risk vs. benefit exercise, between losing one's license and hearing that engine races to the redline!

If you have the chance to come across a Singer, you can perform this one-finger test to appreciate the depth of engineering: put your forefinger on the rear mirror adjustment stick and move it around…and feel that smooth oil-slick precision movement. If someone can spend that much effort to perfect the control of a mirror, imagine what the rest of the car is like…

車主的話：

對於 Singer 著名的「restomod」（復修改裝）964，汽車界眾多評測已經言盡它的特性。也許從車主的角度來看，我可以分享其復修改裝的轉變，因為我曾駕駛過改裝前的原裝 964 Targa。

雖然沒人指責過保時捷有任何「拙劣」的工程，但 Singer 的改造令它耳目一新。

第一印象是方向盤：更加敏銳和緊湊。波箱具有彈簧螺絲般精密的運作。車身控制和剎車性能達到了另一個水平……還有那個引擎：現在是 4.0 公升容量，帶有令人震慄的風冷聲音。每次駕駛都是一次風險與收益的對賭，要在保住駕駛執照與聆聽引擎疾馳至紅線之間取得平衡！

如果你有機會遇見一輛 Singer，你可以試做這項「單指測試」，以欣賞其深厚的工程技術：把你的食指放在後視鏡的調整桿上，並向四周移動……感受那平滑的精確運轉。如果有人能花這麼多心思來完善一個後視鏡的控制，想像一下整輛車的其餘部份會是怎樣的……

Porsche 保時捷 964 Targa
Reimagined by Singer Vehicle Design
(1990)

Singer is a Californian company that specialises in "restomodding" the Porsche 964 model – they create their vision of what a top-spec 964 would look like if it were made today. The Singer we are reviewing here is known as "HK15", meaning it is the 15th Singer for Hong Kong. It started out life as a 1990 964 Targa Tiptronic.

As with all Singers, all the body panels, aside from the doors, have been replaced by carbon fibre panels. The wheels are wide retro-Fuchs wheels to go with the widened rear fenders. The brakes are original 993 Turbo brakes which are more than ample for the lightweight car (Singer says they saved 500 pounds from the original 964). For the engine, Singer retains the original 964 block but increased the capacity to 4.0 litres along with other internal enhancements. As a result, the car has about 390HP now. Singer claims that all their cars would at most only have a 3 HP discrepancy as all Singer engines were tuned meticulously. Most Singers have an intake manifold taken from the 997 GT3 which, while it looks great, I have always thought it did not look period correct. However, by the time this owner started picking options for his car, Singer released their "Velocity Stack Trumpet" intakes which look superb and are much more fitting, optically.

Singer's official motto is "Everything is important". I will say this; everywhere you look in the car it is an intentional presentation. Everything, like the interior leather, the dials, the nickel-plated rearview mirrors etc. are all presented beautifully and would make a great photo regardless of what camera you use. This is particularly true with the engine bay – surrounded

Singer 是一家位於加利福尼亞州、專門「復修改裝」保時捷 964 現代型號的公司。他們創造了一輛他們理想的最高規格 964 版本。在這裏評測的 Singer 被稱為「HK15」，意思是它乃第 15 輛來到香港的 Singer。它原本是一輛 1990 年的 964 Targa Tiptronic。

與所有 Singer 一樣，除了車門，所有車身面板都被碳纖維面板取代。車輛配有寬大的復古 Fuchs 輪圈，以配合加寬的後沙板。剎車系統是原裝的 993 Turbo 剎車系統，對於這輛輕量車來說完全足夠（Singer 稱他們比原始 964 車型減重 500 磅）。就引擎而言，Singer 保留了原始的 964 氣缸，但將容量提高至 4.0 公升，同時增強了其他內部設備。因此，車輛現在的馬力約為 390 匹。Singer 稱他們所有車輛的引擎調校精確，馬力最多只會有 3 匹的差異。大多數 Singer 車型採用了來自 997 GT3 的進氣箱，雖然看上去很棒，但我總覺得它不合時宜。然而，當這位車主開始為他的車輛挑選項目時，Singer 推出了「Velocity Stack Trumpet」進氣管道，看起來非常出色，更符合視覺效果。

Singer 的官方格言是「一切都重要」。我要說的是：車內的每個角落都是刻意精心安排的。無論是內飾皮革、儀錶盤、鍍鎳後視鏡等，所有東西都呈現出華麗的效果，無論你使用哪種相機都可以拍出很棒的照片。尤其是引擎艙——周圍都是海洋級皮革，可承受引擎的熱量。你可以將完美佈置的引擎艙拿出來放在客廳中央作為藝術品展示，一點也不會顯得格格不入。

談談駕駛體驗——真是令人嘆為觀止！你首先會注意到，也是整個駕駛過程中佔據你感官的，就是它發出的聲音。Singer 將水平對向 6 缸引擎提升到賽車級水平。這個引擎的聲音讓我想起 1990 年代澳門格蘭披治大賽跑道上電視轉播 964 賽車的聲音。

by marine-grade leather to withstand the engine heat. You can pull out the perfectly laid out engine bay and display it in the middle of a living room as an art piece and it won't look out of place one bit.

Now on the driving – it is mind-blowing! The first thing you notice, and the thing that will occupy your senses for the entire driving experience, is the sound it makes. Singer has taken the flat-six engine to a racing level. The engine sound really reminds me of the 964 Cup racers that raced through the Macao Grand Prix circuit on television back in the 1990s. The clutch and gear changes are easy and feel great and the pedals encourage heel and toeing for every downshift. The handling also feels very firm and direct, unlike the stock 964 I tried many years ago which felt rather dull. The Ohlins suspensions are firm but not uncomfortable. It is a car that just makes you want to step on it again and again, just to get that rush through all your senses. It is a remarkable experience.

And now I am a convert. I understand why people would pay so much to create a Singer. The engine and chassis, while enhanced, are still from a classic car and therefore retain the rawness and direct feeling that you no longer get from modern cars. Modern cars are simply too high-tech that they will never be able to give you the same rush and feel.

I have always preferred Ferrari's over Porsche's. However, if there is one dream Porsche that I can have, it would be the Singer…

離合器和轉波裝置都很容易操作且感覺良好，每次轉低波時踏板都會鼓勵腳趾動作。操控感非常堅實且直接，不像多年前我試駕的原裝 964 車型，感覺相當平淡。Ohlins 避震系統堅實而不會讓人感到不適。這是一輛讓你不禁想一次又一次踩下油門的車，為了讓你所有的感官都獲得衝刺感。這是一個非凡的體驗。

我現在已成了它的信徒。我理解為何人們會花那麼多錢來打造一輛 Singer。引擎和底盤雖然得到加強，但畢竟來自一部老爺車，因此保留了現代汽車所沒有的原始感和直接感。現代汽車科技太高，永遠無法給你相同的激情和感受。

我一直喜歡法拉利多於保時捷。然而，如果我能擁有一輛夢想中的保時捷，那必定是 Singer……

Production Year: 1998
Engine: Fuel injected 2.2 turbocharged flat-4; 280HP
Total Production: 424 units

生產年份： 1998
引擎：燃油噴注 2.2 渦輪增壓水平對向 4 缸；280 匹馬力
總產量：424 輛

Owner's remarks:

The 22B brings back so many memories from my uni days. I was lucky enough to have a basic Impreza WRX back in 1999 and had always dreamt of having a 22B one day. I feel young again when I drive my 22B now.

車主的話：

22B 讓我想起大學時代的種種回憶。我幸運地在 1999 年擁有了一輛基本版的 Impreza WRX，並一直夢想着有朝一日能擁有一輛 22B。現在開着我的 22B，我感覺自己重返年輕時代。

Subaru 富士
Impreza WRX 22B STi (1998)

The Subaru 22B STi was created in 1998 to celebrate Subaru's 40th anniversary as well as their 3rd consecutive win of the World Rally Championship. Only 400 units were made for the Japanese domestic market initially, but another 24 were released shortly after specifically for the UK and Australian markets due to popular demand. The 22B can be considered as the first true special and limited edition of the Subaru STi line up, which kicked off generations of subsequent special edition models that we are familiar with today, such as the S209 and Spec-C models.

Improvements over the regular STi model were not as over the top as today's special editions, they were subtle but significant. Engine improvements included a different turbo and other internal upgrades, most notable of which was the increase of capacity from 2.0 to 2.2 litres. Bilstein made a set of suspensions specifically for the 22B and the brakes were Subaru's in-house four piston calipers which are small and frankly laughable by today's standards, but they were the brakes to have back in the late 1990s. The exterior modifications are what excite most enthusiasts even today: tailor-made front and rear bumpers just for the 22B, a huge adjustable rear wing, and beautiful period BBS rims in gold giving the car just the right aggressive stance. However, by far the most important exterior upgrade was the front and rear fenders, widened by about 3.5 inches, making it the most recognisable and defining feature of this special model.

The car uses Subaru's legendary boxer engine, four cylinders with a single turbo, which claimed to produce only 280HP but likely to be around 300-

富士 22B STi 於 1998 年面世，以慶祝車廠的 40 週年紀念，以及他們連續第三次贏得世界拉力錦標賽冠軍。最初只生產了 400 輛供日本國內市場使用，但由於廣受歡迎，不久後又推出另外 24 輛，特別供應給英國和澳洲市場。22B 可被視為富士 STi 系列的第一個真正特別和限量版本，並衍生出我們今天熟悉的一系列特別版車型，如 S209 和 Spec-C 等。

與現在的特別版相比，22B 相對於普通 STi 車型上的改進並沒有那麼誇張，而是細微而顯著的。引擎的改進包括不同的渦輪和其他內部升級，其中最值得注意的是將排氣量從 2.0 公升增加到 2.2 公升。Bilstein 為 22B 專門製作了一套避震系統，而剎車系統則採用了富士自家製的四活塞卡鉗，與現代標準相比或許顯得有點小及可笑，但在上世紀 90 年代它們是最受追捧的剎車系統。對於熱愛改裝的車迷來說，外觀的修改仍然是最令人興奮的：為 22B 度身定製的前後保險桿、巨大的可調節後翼，以及華麗的 BBS 金色輪圈，使車輛呈現出其恰到好處。然而，最重要的外部升級無疑是前後沙板，擴寬了約 3.5 英寸，成為這款特殊車型最為人熟知和突出的特點。

這輛車採用富士傳奇的對沖引擎，四缸單渦輪，宣稱只生產 280 匹馬力，但實際可能有 300-320 匹馬力左右（當時的日本製造商必須遵守一份「君子協定」，即所有車型限制在 280 匹馬力，以防止飛車文化）。這是在過度使用碳纖維的時代之前（事實上，當時並沒有使用碳纖維），因此減重不是 22B 的主要目標，實際上這些日本拉力跑車由始至終也不算重（只有約 1,300 公斤）。

20 世紀 90 年代的富士 WRX STi 屬於日本跑車黃金時代的產物，與三菱 Evolution 和日產 GTR 等車型並列。由於它們是如此造工精湛的車輛，它們的引擎可能比法拉利、林寶堅尼和保時捷等品牌的

320HP instead (Japanese manufacturers at the time had to enter into this "gentlemen's agreement" where all their cars are limited to 280HP so as to discourage boy racer culture). This was before the days of excessive carbon fibre use (in fact, none was used), so weight saving was not a big part of the 22B's agenda, although these Japanese rally racers were never heavy to begin with (around 1,300KG only).

The nineties-noughties Subaru WRX STi belongs to the prime era of Japanese sports cars, joining the likes of the Mitsubishi Evolution and the Nissan GTR. This is because they were such sophisticated packages – their engines might be smaller than the likes of Ferrari's, Lamborghini's, and Porsche's, but they were able to use the 280HP so efficiently making it very accessible to everyday drivers. This was, for the most part, helped by their technological ingenuity. All had four-wheel drive and cars like the Mitsubishi Evolution 6, for example, had the active yaw control system which was one of the earliest iterations of electronic driver aids that we are so used to today. This means that for an ordinary driver like myself, I am able to extract the performance out of these hero JDM cars a lot easier than its European counterparts.

Full power in the 22B comes in at about 3,400RPM making low end power and progression very good, but top end lacks a bit, with not much going on after 5,000RPM or so. The gears are short too, making it perfect for mountain roads of Hong Kong without any long straights. As with most cars in the 1990s, this car's size is compact. Together with its sophisticated four-wheel drive system, it makes the car very easy to throw around corners confidently. With values of the 22B having skyrocketed to well over HK$2 million in the last few years however, it did not take long before I voluntarily eased off the throttle and returned the car back to its generous owner, with a big smile on my face…

引擎小，但能夠將 280 匹馬力的效率發揮得非常出色，對普通駕駛者來說更易於駕駛。這在很大程度上歸功於它們的技術創新。所有車型都配備四輪驅動系統，例如三菱 Evolution 6 就配備了主動式舵角控制系統，這是最早的電子駕駛輔助技術之一，今天我們已經非常熟悉。這意味着對於像我這樣的普通駕駛者來說，比起其他歐洲跑車，我能夠更容易地發揮這些英雄級日本車的性能。

22B 的最高性能在約每分鐘 3,400 轉時達到，使低速動力和漸進性非常圓滿，但高轉速時較為缺乏，至每分鐘 5,000 轉後的表現不太明顯。這款車的波段比較短，非常適合香港缺少太長直線路段的山路。和 1990 年代的大多數車一樣，這款車的尺寸相對小，再加上其精密的四輪驅動系統，使這款車在轉彎時非常穩定。然而，隨着 22B 的身價在過去幾年急劇上漲至超過 200 萬港元，不用多久，我就主動鬆開油門，笑意盈盈地把車還給慷慨的車主……

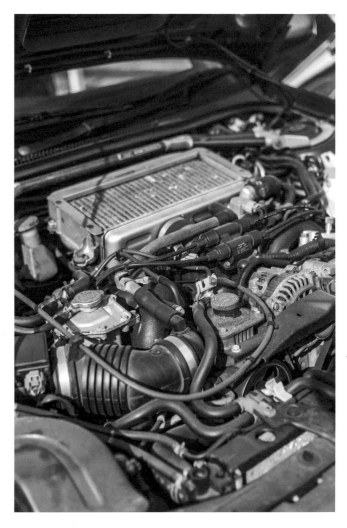

Production Years: 1995-1997
Engine: 4.7 V12; 513HP
Total Production: 349 units

生產年份：1995-1997
引擎：4.7 V12；513 匹馬力
總產量：349 輛

Ferrari 法拉利
F50 RHD 右軚版
(1995)

Throughout this book, I have only included reviews of cars that I have tested and driven before. However, for this bonus review, I will make an exception because of how extraordinarily special this car is. All true petrol heads have that one "unicorn" dream car that, although they know they will never own, they will nevertheless be forever loyal to. That car for me is the Ferrari F50 – forever my unattainable dream car.

Like its predecessor – the Ferrari F40 which I have had the pleasure of properly reviewing (see page 104) – the Ferrari F50 is part of the Ferrari "Big 5" with state-of-the-art Formula 1 technology infused into it at the time. Its engine is derived directly from the Ferrari 641 Formula One racer and its body has extensive carbon-fibre use, which is rare for production road cars at the time.

With only 349 units made, the F50 is one of the rarest Big 5 Ferrari made, with only the 288 GTO being rarer. The car shown here, however, is not an ordinary F50, because it is a right-hand drive version. As with all Big 5 Ferrari's, Ferrari only officially produced them in left-hand drive layout, which is friendlier for Europe and US markets. The first owner of this F50, however, is none other than the Sultan of Brunei, who is known for collecting vast number of cars, most of which were custom made for him by the manufacturers. This F50 was no exception, whereby the Sultan had ordered it in right hand drive layout when new. However, the conversion from left-hand drive to right-hand drive layout was apparently done by Pininfarina, the design house that designed the F50, rather than Ferrari themselves.

There are various claims of how many right-hand drive F50's there are in the world, ranging from 3 to 8. Whatever the truth is, it is indisputable that this is an extremely rare and unique car. This is the only known right hand drive F50 in Hong Kong. The owner acquired it from the UK in around 2011 and thankfully, registered the car in Hong Kong, which means that it comes out reasonably frequently. The photos displayed here are from a Ferrari morning drive that I organised in January 2023. Although I did not get to drive my ultimate dream car, just being in its presence and driving alongside it was a privilege and a memory that would stay with me forever.

這本書僅收錄我曾測試並駕駛過的汽車的評測。然而，這篇額外評測例外。我雖沒有親自駕駛過，但因為這款汽車實在太特別了。所有真正車迷心中，都有一款遙不可及的夢想之車，即使他們知道永遠不可能擁有，但仍然對它從一而終。對我來說，這輛車就是法拉利 F50——我永遠無法得到的夢想之車。

就像它的前輩——我曾有幸仔細評測的法拉利 F40（見第 104 頁）——法拉利 F50 也是當時融入了最先進一級方程式技術的法拉利「Big 5」車型之一。它的引擎直接源自法拉利 641 一級方程式賽車，其車體廣泛使用碳纖維，在當時的量產汽車中非常罕見。

F50 僅生產了 349 輛，是最罕見的法拉利 Big 5 車型之一，僅次於 288 GTO。然而，這裏展示的並不是普通的 F50，因為它是右軚版。跟所有法拉利 Big 5 一樣，官方只生產左軚版車型，以迎合歐美市場的需求。然而，這輛 F50 的第一位車主卻是汶萊蘇丹，他以收集大量汽車著稱，其中大多數是由生產商為他特別定製的。而這輛 F50 也不例外，蘇丹在購買新車時就要求是右軚版。然而，從左軚換成右軚的工序顯然是由設計 F50 的 Pininfarina 公司而不是由法拉利完成的。

對於全球有多少右軚版的 F50 眾說紛紜，從 3 輛到 8 輛不等。無論真相如何，這輛 F50 都是一輛極其罕見且獨特的汽車，也是香港唯一已知的右軚版 F50。車主約於 2011 年從英國購入它，而且幸運地，這輛車在香港註冊，意味着它會頻繁地在街上出現。這裏展示的照片是我於 2023 年 1 月組織的法拉利晨駕活動中拍攝的。雖然我未能親自駕駛這輛我夢寐以求的車，但能夠親臨其境並與它並肩而行已經是一種榮幸，這將成為我永遠的回憶。

Team bios 團隊簡介

Alex Wilson

When Justin came to a group of us and said he wanted to create YouTube content, I was happy to help.

I work in the broadcasting and corporate video field and have a company. So, during the slow times, there is the opportunity for me to be a cameraman and editor, and to learn about action cameras and new techniques.

Editing is time-consuming, but as this is a hobby, it is no problem. Volunteer work is frequently more satisfying than paid work.

I have enjoyed meeting owners and sharing a joint mission to try to tell stories about cars and showcase my adopted home Hong Kong.

當 Justin（呂璟豪）來找我，説他想創建 YouTube 內容時，我很高興可以幫忙。

我在廣播和企業拍攝領域工作，並開設了一家公司。所以，我在閒暇時有機會成為攝影師和編輯，學習有關動作攝影機和新技術的知識。

編輯工作非常耗時，但由於車是我的愛好，所以問題不大。義務工作通常比受薪工作更令人有滿足感。

我很喜歡與車主見面，與他們一同講述有關汽車的故事，並展示我所居住的家——香港。

Dave Chung 鍾致偉

My first car was a VW Polo in glorious bright yellow, so you could say I have not always had a passion for cars!

Helping make InstacarHK has certainly allowed me to experience a bunch of cars that I would not have been able to access otherwise, and I have loved every minute of it.

As well as meeting other owners and exchanging stories about our car experiences, filming for InstacarHK has also allowed me to experiment with different angle and styles of story-telling.

It has been a wonderful journey with friends and one that I hope does not end.

我擁有的第一輛車是亮黃色的福士 Polo，你可以説我並非一向對汽車充滿熱情！

協助製作 InstacarHK 確實讓我有機會體驗到一些我原本無法接觸的汽車，而且拍攝時的每一分秒我也喜歡。

除了與其他車主見面，交流有關汽車經歷的故事之外，為 InstacarHK 拍攝也讓我嘗試不同的敍事角度和風格。

這是一段與朋友共度的美妙旅程，希望永遠不會結束。

Alex Chan 陳維智

It is an offer you could not refuse! That was when Justin offered me a seat in InstacarHK to review and take videos of all these classics in metal and flesh. An offer that gives you close encounters with super rare supercars and classic cars. Being a supercar and classic car enthusiast, it is more like Christmas every weekend.

In the team, my job is driving the camera car: keeping the camera car in the best position for the camera crew to shoot rolling videos and stills according to script.

During the process, I also acquired a small skill in flying a drone, adding to the videos a new dimension of aerial shots and drone chases.

Having good company with friends (teammates) and cars on weekends, what else could one ask for!

這個機會你不能拒絕！當 Justin 邀請我加入 InstacarHK，評測和拍攝這些充滿歷史和魅力的老爺車時，我欣然接受。這個機會讓你可近距離接觸十分罕見的超級跑車和老爺車。作為一個超跑和老爺車愛好者，每個拍攝的週末都像在過聖誕節。

在團隊中，我負責開車協助拍攝：把車駛至最佳位置，讓攝影師們可以根據劇本拍攝連續影片和硬照。

在拍攝過程中，我還掌握了駕駛無人機的小技巧，為影片增添了全新的空中鏡頭和無人機追逐片段。

在週末能與朋友（隊友）和汽車一起，夫復何求！

Adhiraj Rathore

Adhiraj Rathore has been an automotive photographer for just under 10 years and is the founder of one of Hong Kong's biggest automotive Instagram pages "Super Cars of Hong Kong".

Since very young, Adhiraj has had a really strong passion and love towards cars and anything relating to them. Growing up in Hong Kong, he realised at a young age that Hong Kong has an extremely strong car culture with everything to offer varying from the rarest classics to the newest super/hypercars. This led him to borrow a friend's camera for the first time 10 years ago to attend his first car meet. The rest was history. This has led him to become one of Hong Kong's most iconic automotive photographers and a well-known photographer worldwide.

Companies such as Apollo Automobili and DeTamoso regularly commission Adhiraj to help shoot their newest models both in Hong Kong and Europe. Adhiraj has also been a member of the "InstacarHK" team since the very beginning helping to bring more of Hong Kong's car scene to both the local and international car communities. With his passion for both classics and modern cars, this is a perfect fit.

Adhiraj Rathore 是一名從事汽車攝影工作近 10 年的專業攝影師，也是香港最大汽車 Instagram 專頁「Super Cars of Hong Kong」的創始人。

他從幼時就對汽車和與之相關的一切產生濃厚的熱情和熱愛。他在香港長大，很早就意識到香港有着非常濃厚的汽車文化，從最罕見的老爺車到最新的超級跑車，應有盡有。這促使他在 10 年前第一次借用朋友的相機參加了人生首次汽車聚會。這令他成為香港最具代表性的汽車攝影師之一，也成為世界知名的攝影師。

Apollo Automobili 和 DeTamoso 等公司經常委託 Adhiraj 拍攝在香港和歐洲的最新車型。Adhiraj 從一開始就是「InstacarHK」的隊員，協助將更多香港的汽車文化帶給本地和國際汽車社群。加上他對老爺車和現代車都充滿熱情，可說是天作之合。

Martin Lee 李啟恩（IG：@visualspassport）

Martin is an automotive and travel photographer based in Hong Kong. He began his photography journey with his first DSLR back in 2008 but really got his photography going after opening his Instagram account in 2016 and sharing photos on a daily basis. He has built a reputation internationally for his drone photography amassing more than 45k followers, and eventually his passion in motorsport and supercars gradually became a part of his photographic interests.

Through his friend – Adhiraj, he started helping the InstacarHK team out with drone videos and shooting still photos. Eventually, he became part of the core team, after shooting various rare classics including the Ferrari F40, Theon Design 964 restomod, and the AC Cobra.

Since integrating automotive subjects into his photography work in 2021, he has been commissioned by major automotive brands and local dealerships to create automotive content in Hong Kong. His clients include Mercedes-Benz HK, Hyundai-N Worldwide and Blackbird Maserati, and he has been commissioned to shoot a variety of automobiles, including the highly exclusive Mercedes-AMG ONE.

李啟恩是一位駐守香港的汽車和旅行攝影師。早在 2008 年，他就用第一台單反相機展開了他的攝影之旅，一直到 2016 年開設 Instagram 賬號並每天分享照片後，他的攝影生涯才真正開始。他以無人機拍攝而在國際上享有盛譽，擁有超過 45,000 名粉絲，後來他對賽車運動和超級跑車的熱情逐漸成為他攝影興趣的一部份。

透過朋友 Adhiraj 的介紹，他開始協助 InstacarHK 團隊拍攝無人機影片和硬照。他最終成為團隊的核心成員，參與拍攝包括法拉利 F40、Theon Design 964 Restomod 和 AC Cobra 等多款罕有老爺車型。

自 2021 年將汽車題材融入攝影作品以來，他已經接受多家主要汽車品牌和本地經銷商的委託，在香港創建汽車內容。他的客戶包括 Mercedes-Benz HK、Hyundai-N Worldwide 和 Blackbird Maserati，並獲邀拍攝各種汽車，包括極為獨特的 Mercedes-AMG ONE。

Icy J - @icy95

Cord Krohn 雍浩

Cord Krohn is a professional photographer who takes portraits by trade and is most passionate about car photography – more specifically capturing Hong Kong's unique and diverse car culture. In his early 20s, he dabbled in photography, but it was in 2020, thanks to his masterful teacher, Zahra Darvishian, that he realised his calling. The images of Hong Kong's talented automotive photography team, Black Cygnus, inspired him to keep improving.

With a true love for cars, Cord enjoys car spotting at any opportunity and often spends his weekends capturing Hong Kong's passionate drivers, particularly on their early Sunday morning drives. Cord hopes to support local car enthusiasts in his own way for years to come.

雍浩是一名專業攝影師，以人像攝影為主。他亦對汽車攝影充滿熱情，特別是捕捉香港獨特多樣的汽車文化。他二十出頭時曾嘗試過攝影，但直到 2020 年，多得他優秀的老師 Zahra Darvishian 指導，他才醒覺攝影是他的使命。才華橫溢的香港汽車攝影團隊 Black Cygnus 的作品激勵他不斷進步。

雍浩熱愛汽車，隨時都喜歡在街上用相機捕獲汽車，通常在週末拍攝參與晨駕活動的熱情香港車主。他希望能夠在未來幾年繼續以個人的方式支持本地車迷。

Berton Chang 張銘良

Berton has been in the photography industry since 2007 and is regularly commissioned for portraiture and editorial projects. His work with InstacarHK is his first exposure to automotive photography which has been "a welcome departure" from his day-to-day work.

張銘良從 2007 年起加入攝影行業，經常受委託進行人像攝影和編輯項目。他與 InstacarHK 的合作讓他首次接觸汽車攝影，他認為這是「一個令人愉快的告別」，使他有機會離開日常工作。

From left to right: Martin Lee, Justin Lui (Author), Alex Chan, Owner of F40, Dave Chung, Adhiraj Rathore, Alex Wilson

由左至右：李啟恩、呂璟豪（作者）、陳維智、F40 車主、鍾致偉、Adhiraj Rathore、Alex Wilson

www.cosmosbooks.com.hk

Spectacular Cars of Hong Kong
——An InstacarHK Journey

經典的魅力
——InstacarHK 試駕之旅

Author: Justin Lui
Organiser: Chris Cheung
Editor: K.F. Kwok
Designer: Anthony Kwok

作者：呂璟豪
策劃：張宇程
責任編輯：郭坤輝
美術編輯：郭志民

Published by Cosmos Books Ltd.
Head Office:
11/F, Sun Hing Industrial Building,
46 Wong Chuk Hang Road, Hong Kong
Tel: 2528 3671 Fax: 2865 2609
Bookstore:
Basement, 30 Johnston Road, Wanchai, Hong Kong
Tel: 2865 0708 Fax: 2861 1541

出版：
天地圖書有限公司
香港黃竹坑道 46 號
新興工業大廈 11 樓（總寫字樓）
電話：2528 3671 傳真：2865 2609
香港灣仔莊士敦道 30 號地庫（門市部）
電話：2865 0708 傳真：2861 1541

Printed by Elegance Printing & Book Binding Co., Ltd.
Flat A, 4/F, Hoi Bun Industrial Building, 6 Wing Yip Street,
Kwun Tong, Hong Kong
Tel: 2342 0109 Fax: 2790 3614

印刷：
美雅印刷製本有限公司
香港九龍觀塘榮業街 6 號海濱工業大廈 4 樓 A 室
電話：2342 0109 傳真：2790 3614

Distributed by SUP Retail (Hong Kong) Limited
16/F, Tsuen Wan Industrial Centre, 220-248 Texaco Road,
Tsuen Wan, N.T., Hong Kong
Tel: 2150 2100 Fax: 2407 3062

發行：
聯合新零售（香港）有限公司
香港新界荃灣德士古道 220-248 號荃灣工業中心 16 樓
電話：2150 2100 傳真：2407 3062

First published in November, 2023, Hong Kong
© COSMOS BOOKS LTD. 2023

出版日期：2023 年 11 月 / 初版・香港
© COSMOS BOOKS LTD. 2023

國際書號：978-988-8551-16-3